AF530652

To Surju, With Love

Jaiwanti Dimri is a bilingual writer, critic and translator. A recipient of the Arya Smriti Samman, Kitabghar (2002), in the genre of Hindi short story, her stories have been published in national journals, magazines and anthologies, and translated into English, Telugu and Marathi. A former professor of English at Himachal Pradesh University, Shimla, she has taught in Nigeria, Bhutan and the US, and has also been a fellow of the Indian Institute of Advanced Study, Shimla. Her published works include: *The Inner Eye and Other Stories* (2016); *Images and Representation of the Rural Woman: A Study of the Selected Novels of Indian Women Writers* (2012); *The Drukpa Mystique: Bhutan in 21st Century* (2004); *Ernest Hemingway: A Critical Study of His Short Stories and Non-Fiction* (1994); two novellas in Hindi, *Pinddaan* (2012) and *Surju Ke Naam* (2006); two Hindi short story collections, *Gagar Bhar Paani* (2004) and *Dusra Narak Kund* (2004); and *Sahastra Netradhari Nayak* (2009), a Hindi translation of Bhutanese writer Karma Ura's novel *The Hero with a Thousand Eyes*. Jaiwanti Dimri lives in Dehradun.

To Surju, With Love

Transcreated from the original Hindi
by the author

Jaiwanti Dimri

Orient BlackSwan

TO SURJU, WITH LOVE

ORIENT BLACKSWAN PRIVATE LIMITED

Registered Office
3-6-752 Himayatnagar, Hyderabad 500 029, Telangana, India
e-mail: centraloffice@orientblackswan.com

Other Offices
Bengaluru, Bhopal, Chennai, Guwahati, Hyderabad,
Jaipur, Kolkata, Lucknow, Mumbai, New Delhi,
Noida, Patna, Vijayawada

Originally published in Hindi as *Surju Ke Naam* (New Delhi: Jnanpith, 2006).

First published by Orient Blackswan Pvt. Ltd. 2017

ISBN 978-93-86296-98-6

Typeset in
Adobe Jenson Pro 11.5/14.2
by Le Studio Graphique, Gurgaon 122 001

024598

15122016

Printed in India at
B. B. Press
Noida

Published by
Orient Blackswan Private Limited
3-6-752 Himayatnagar, Hyderabad 500 029, Telangana, India
e-mail: info@orientblackswan.com

Contents

Acknowledgements

I owe a debt of gratitude, love and affection to the following people, places and organisations that have, in explicit and implicit ways, contributed to the making of this book.

I express my sincere gratitude to the Government of India and the Royal Government of Bhutan for offering me the opportunity to work in Bhutan under the aegis of the Colombo Plan in 1997–1999.

I salute all those people whose heard and unheard melodies are recollected in this book.

Lastly, I thank Orient BlackSwan for publishing this novella.

Jaiwanti Dimri

Introduction

This narrative is located in a small town named Kanglung in eastern Bhutan. Druk Yul, or the Land of the Peaceful Dragon as the Drukpas call it, comprises two words in Dzongkha, the national language of Bhutan: *druk* [thunder dragon] and *yul* [land]. The Bhutanese are called Drukpas by virtue of their faith in the Thunder Dragon, which is a powerful religious symbol for them. The country celebrated its 108th National Day as a democratic monarchy on 17 December 2015. On 14 December 2006, the fifth king of Bhutan, His Majesty Jigme Singye Wangchuk abdicated the throne in favour of the Crown Prince, the Tongsa Penlop [Governor] Jigme Khesar Namgyel Wangchuk, who succeeded him. Two years later on 7 November 2008, with his coronation as the sixth king of Bhutan, or Druk Gyalpo, the country registered a historic shift to the democratic form of monarchy after a hundred years of Buddhist monarchical rule and three hundred and fifty years of theocratic monarchy in the Himalayan region.

Nestled in the foothills of the eastern Himalayas, with its magnificent and panoramic landscapes, lush valleys, snow-clad mountains, deep gorges, rivers and waterfalls, home to a diverse and unique fauna and flora, Bhutan, which was till late the only Buddhist monarchy in the Himalayan region, has truly been blessed with God's plenty. In this age of globalisation, consumerism, market economy and cut-throat competition, Bhutan has emerged as an exemplary model of 'restricted eco-friendly exotic tourism' and aptly declared as one of the ten global hotspots for the conservation of biodiversity. The numerous Buddhist temples, monasteries, stupas, prayer flags and rotating prayer wheels around every corner against the backdrop of resplendent natural beauty impart a distinctive ambience to this small Himalayan nation and its people. Elsewhere, I have preferred to describe this unique harmony between the land and its people as the quality of mystique.

During my two-year memorable stay in Bhutan in 1997–1999 under the aegis of the Colombo Plan, I could not only fulfill my professional commitments but, owing to the unusual serenity of the surroundings, was also able to engage with my creative pursuits, which often get neglected due to academic and professional constraints. Three of my books *The Drukpa Mystique: Bhutan in 21st Century* (2004), *Sahastra Netradhari Nayak* (2009), a Hindi translation of Bhutanese writer Karma Ura's debutante novel *The Hero with a Thousand Eyes*, and *Surju Ke Naam* (2006), a Hindi novella, I owe to the privileged and rare opportunity of watching this unique country and its people from close quarters during my stay in Bhutan. With the publication of *To Surju, With Love*, I could not have asked for more.

The Bhutanese are immensely proud of their history as an independent Buddhist nation which successfully thwarted repeated attempts of the British to subdue and colonise them. Rooted firmly in its national and cultural heritage as well as its ecological strength, Bhutan is committed to the paradigm of National Gross Happiness (NGH) and to prioritising quality of life in terms of the human values of kindness, equality and humanity. Implicit in the NGH paradigm is the quintessence of the Buddhist philosophy of life nurtured over decades amidst the awe-inspiring and rugged Himalayan landscape. This Land of the Thunder Dragon is the last country in the world to follow the Mahayana form of Buddhism, as practiced by the Kagyu sect.

In sharp contrast to the mesmerizing natural beauty of Bhutan which forms the backdrop of *To Surju, With Love*, the narrative engages with the disturbing submerged realities of the lives of subaltern Indians in this landlocked country. The large number of Indian labourers working on construction sites in remote corners and borders of the country would meet the defining variables of the Gramscian subaltern. One such subaltern in terms of identity, money, class and gender is Sukurmani, the protagonist of this novella. As an illiterate, unskilled labourer of tribal origin, a single parent and an illegal, displaced cross-border migrant, she is located virtually on the margin of margins. On the surface of it, her everyday ordeals and struggles may seem localised. But closer enquiry reveals a more complex web of reality, of power dynamics with larger political and socio-economic dimensions wherein the personal becomes political and the lives of those on the margins are impacted by policies framed and implemented at the national and international level. Sukurmani is just a metaphor for the countless Sukurmanis caught in the diasporic web, and her predicament cannot and must not be dismissed or undermined as individual or local, and thus of lesser magnitude in the larger national or global context.

In recent years, the large-scale internal and external migration of people within and outside the borders of the country has given rise to new problems and the formation of new equations that posit the need to redefine and revisit the constructs of nation, state and identity. Such multidimensional migration not only problematises the concept of a homogenised nation and history as a metanarrative, it also creates what Salman Rushdie describes as a 'dislocated people' who tend to define themselves by their 'Otherness,' who root themselves in ideas rather than in places, and in memories as much as in ideas. Benedict Anderson's critique of nation in *Imagined Communities* also takes cognisance of such large-scale cross-border migrations.

Bhutan as a buffer state between China and India holds a strategically significant position for both the Asian countries. Prime Minister Narendra Modi's first foreign visit, after assuming office in 2014, to this Himalayan state is evidence of that. The

Government of India has been a generous contributor to the overall development of Bhutan in all spheres, and the two countries share an old friendship based on mutual cooperation and trust. The Colombo Plan—under which I served in Sherubtse College, Kanglung, the present University of Bhutan—is one such project that aims to promote technical cooperation amongst the SAARC nations. The Indian Army and the General Reserve Engineering Force (GREF), which is part of the Border Roads Organisation (BRO,) have long been engaged in the construction of roads, dams and bridges across Bhutan, and thus have a visible presence there.

For these big construction projects in Bhutan, while legally recruited Indian labourers usually comprise bulk of the work force, many illegal Bangladeshi and Indian migrants also succeed in finding work at these construction sites under an assumed 'pan-Indian' identity. Sukurmani, the protagonist, is one such illegal Indian migrant labourer-turned domestic help, toiling day and night for survival. Of the multiple identities attached to her—poor, widow, single mother, illegal migrant, illiterate, ditched lover, maidservant—none is completely definitive or contains the woman called Sukurmani because each of these identities is circumstantial and therefore transient; in fact even the name we know her by is not her own.

Like his mother, Surju, Sukurmani's four-year old son is also a passive recipient of circumstances which are not of his making. As a cross-border illegal migrant's son, he cannot escape the context of his birth. This lesser known subaltern child in the nation state often catches the attention of ideologues, film makers, writers and social welfare organisations. Devendra Satyarthi's Nobel-winning 'Save Childhood' campaign is a grim reminder of the continued exploitation of children like Surju who, being poor and caught between borders but belonging nowhere, often become the worst targets of child abuse, child trafficking and child labour. The role of the nation state with regard to these most vulnerable and disempowered members of poor, migrant, diasporic populations is polemically connected with the paradigmatic issues of nation, cross-border migration, human trafficking and terrorism.

One is familiar with the literary and theoretical debates related to *diaspora*, the Greek term, literally meaning 'completely scattered,' that has come to define modern generations of migrants. Diasporic studies, specifically the postcolonial theories propagated by Frantz Fanon, Ngugi wa Thiong'o, Chinua Achebe, Wole Soyinka, Salman Rushdie, V. S. Naipaul, Homi Bhabha and Gayatri Spivak, are key to understanding the emergent diasporic community formations across the globe in terms of identity, space, the binaries of alienation and assimilation and culture shock. All along while there are deliberations on these diasporic paradigms, I think of Sukurmani, Surju and his half-sister and wonder: where do we fit them into this theoretical framework?

There was a time when the diasporic discourse was by and large male-centric. It is heartening to see that with the persistent engagement of women writers with the issues of gender, identity, class, race and sexuality, the voices of women are no longer located on the margins. However it is also true that much of this diasporic literature is representative of the voices and experiences of the urban, educated diaspora belonging to a privileged class. Subaltern diasporic voices like those of Sukurmani are still located on the peripheries of the dominant canon.

'*Pataa Kahan Hai?*' [Where is the Address?], a short story published in the Hindi magazine *Hans*, was my maiden attempt to comprehend and transmit the subaltern migrant experience from the subjective gendered viewpoint of Sukurmani. The story did not unburden me completely from the inherent sense of unease and disquiet I had long been troubled with, and years later I rewrote the story in the form of a novella *Surju Ke Naam* in Hindi (2006). *To Surju, With Love* is not a verbatim translation of the Hindi novella; transcreation would better describe this endeavour. Embedded in this creative endeavour is also the desire to reach out to a wider readership.

The theme and concerns of *Surju Ke Naam* have certainly not changed, although in its transcreated form it has perhaps turned out to be more elaborate and descriptive. Reproducing the linguistic nuances of a language in terms of local idiom, irony, humour and pithy aphorisms in a translated text is always a challenge. There are no fixed rules and a translator must make and remake his or her own choices, experiment, innovate and take risks, exploring in the process all available options and variables. Literally translating, or to say transmitting the lingua franca of an unlettered polyglot like the protagonist of the novella in standard grammatical English is virtually impossible, and if one attempted to do so, it would flatten and silence much of the jagged beauty of the language. One often came across labourers-turned-domestic helps in Bhutan who spoke and communicated in a language that was a rich and polyphonic mix of Bodo, Dumka, Hindi, English, Bengali, Nepali and the local Sharchopa. I have experimented to the best of my ability to try and capture at least some of the complex charms, nuances and musicality of that colourful language in English.

Like so many across the subcontinent, lettered and unlettered, Sukurmani too has her own limited but unique vocabulary of English words which she pronounces and uses in very specific ways. For Sukurmani's speech, therefore, I have taken the liberty of compromising both spelling and grammar. English words like report, duty, Brother and police, for instance, have become repot, dooty, Bathar and poolis respectively, and italicised on first instance. Her sentences have been deliberately truncated as: 'That I not know'; 'Then I very small'; 'He get *himsa*'; 'Oye baba! He no good!' With a limited vocabulary, one word tends to acquire multiple meanings, as also observed in the case of children. The protagonist's language skills in this narrative could also be said to be compatible with those of a child. Once, a puzzled reader wished to know the exact meaning of Sukurmani's *himsa*. I had no answer. In this novella, too, the word has been retained verbatim. So have indigenous words like *des, raasi, arra, chorten, thu, peesa* (pidgin for the Hindi word *paisa*, meaning money, coin); the meanings have been made clear from the context, and there is also a glossary provided.

As a practicing translator I prefer to adopt the position of a *sahridaya* or compassionate and empathetic reader-translator rather than a matter-of-fact interlocutor or mediator. For I believe it is only when a translator transcends the passivity of an interlocutor and succeeds in internalising the intent of the creator and the text that linguistic and cultural barriers may be overcome, and a translation may be seamlessly done. Only readers can vouchsafe how far I have succeeded in communicating the nuances of the illiterate polyglot protagonist's speech.

I leave the book to the sahridaya reader, who is the best critic and judge.

Jaiwanti Dimri

To Surju, With Love

She still vividly remembers her last day in Kanglung in Druk Yul, this Land of the Peaceful Dragon. The bus had reached the other end of the upper market. It was not yet dawn. The shops were shrouded in fog and pre-dawn darkness. Even the stray dogs that usually crowded the market place were nowhere in sight, neither was their cacophony audible. But down below in the lower market, the round circle of lights illuminating the *zangdopelri*, the temple of Padmasambhava, beloved Guru Rinpoche of the Drukpas, was visible. As she leaned out of the bus window trying to catch a last glimpse of the double-storeyed house further down the road, her eyes grew moist. This market place, these small scattered shops countable on the fingertips, these slate-roofed houses, the terraced fields on the hill slopes, the valley covered with crops of potato and maize—she took in the whole panorama longingly for one last time and inhaled deeply.

The bus moved on past the *chorten*, the chain of stupas at the end of the market meant to obstruct the path of evil spirits. Colourful messenger *dhars*, prayer flags with many different prayers inscribed on them, fluttered in the wind, wishing her bon voyage. She saw the huge *mani*, the prayer wheel in front of the chorten that she had rotated umpteen times. Here, there and everywhere, on the hilltop, at the crossroads, by the roadside, near a *dzong*, a *lhakhang* or a monastery, in the town and in the forest, there would be a chorten, a mani and the dhars. She remembered lines of *The Ballad of Pemi Tshewang Tashi*: 'Up in the lap of the Khujuk mountains where chortens and manis are circumambulated...'

The bus passed by the primary school building, which would soon be abuzz with activity. For the Drukpas or Bhutanese people, functions held in this small school were in no way less than the big *tshechus* or religious festivals. The small boys clad in their *ghos* of brown *matha* and the *kira*-clad girls playing in the school ground would turn their shy, inquisitive glances at you, at times wishing you with a quick bow of the head in passing. The bus turned on the curve, leaving behind the view of the zangdopelri that she used to visit so frequently, circumambulating it along with the devout. She had participated in the *drubchen,* the annual worship rituals which concluded with the blessing ceremony, bowing down before the statue of Guru Rinpoche and receiving the coveted blessings from Lam Netan, the head lama, patiently waiting her turn in the long queue. The lamas, the *anims* or the female monks in the *gompas,* the monasteries and lhakhangs, the temples, the people rotating the manis followed by the sonorous, tinkling sounds, the chanting of mantras, the counting of beads and so much more would from now on become only a part of her reminiscences.

The bus speeding down the road was fast leaving the small town behind. Never again would she board this bus. Never again would she walk past this town. Adieu Kanglung! Adieu Kanglung market! Adieu Sherubtse, the peak of learning! Goodbye, the soft, cold breeze and the soil of this town. It was another matter that her presence or absence would make no difference to this quiet, solitary hill road.

Down below the first bend of the road, the double-storeyed house where Sukurmani occupies a small, dark, dingy room on the ground floor would have a melancholy inmate today. Surju, too, might ask for her. Every evening he would be standing on the threshold, waiting for her. As soon as he caught sight of her approaching figure, he would dart inside to inform his mother. Hiding behind the door he would welcome her with a coy smile. Surju is still a child and may forget her in a day or two. But Sukurmani would perhaps need a little more time to get over her melancholy. It might last till tomorrow, the day after or even a few more days. But the sorrows and miseries of Sukurmani have never relied on tears. Neither does her communication rely on letters or telephone calls. However, at that chaotic moment in her life, Sukurmani had made innumerable calls to Thimphu, all in vain. And she, too, had written a letter to Sukurmani's father, resident of Mejguri, Darranga, a letter she had herself dropped in the letter box.

On second thoughts, she had highlighted the address in bold letters in English. There may not be anyone able to read Hindi in Mejguri village or at the post office in Parki Juli, she thought, but surely someone would be able to read the address in English. But Sarju Tutu did not receive that letter. Or even if he received it, there was no response from him. Perhaps some reader was found who could read out the letter to him, but there was no one available to write a response. She had even considered writing the address in Assamese, but there was no point in writing the letter in Assamese since Sukurmani's father was a Bodo. Until then, she had been so informed.

She had passed through Darranga and the Mela Bazar area of Bodoland so many times in cars and sometimes in buses. Passing through this sensitive area under the Bodo insurgency, she was always gripped by fear. What if some Bodo insurgent emerged from somewhere and fired at them? Her eyes would then watch Bodos on the road: children on their way to school, men and women on cycles and on foot on their way to work. These medium-statured folks seemed simple, unobtrusive and oblivious of their surroundings. Could those dreaded Bodo terrorists be like them?

Those barren, desolate roadside houses with closed shutters and windows—the betel nut, date and palm trees still kept vigil on their empty courtyards. Most of these houses were deserted; it was rumoured that the Indian Army had got them vacated. The sight of the Indian Army trucks and jeeps full of green-uniformed personnel and commandos was more than intimidating, especially that one time when they had stopped her taxi. And the second time was when they were all aboard the Bhutan Post bus, and their bags, suitcases, purses, everything was ordered to be thoroughly searched by the jawans. To feel so exposed and vulnerable in the premises of your own country was a humiliating experience. But later, whenever she passed through that road and closely watched the perspiring faces of those 'agents of state' standing guard in the scorching sun, or soaking wet in the rain, holding the butts of their guns, they seemed in no way less vulnerable and pitiable, constantly on edge and fearful of an impending terrorist attack on them anytime, anywhere.

Throughout the year the roadside fields would be laden with paddy. It was common knowledge, which the newspapers also corroborated, that the people of this region were very poor. But those lush, ripe paddy fields, the rows of coconut, betel nut and palm trees, and the people going their way on the road, engaged in the everyday business of life apparently narrated a different story—they all appeared to be happy and contented beings. She often wondered: who cultivated these fields since all the roadside houses had been converted into barracks? Sukurmani's father, too, must have worked and tilled one of these fields. And Sukurmani's dada, her elder brother must have climbed up one of these palm trees and drunk the palm juice, creating a ruckus.

The thought of Sukurmani reminded her of the letter she had penned to her father Sarju Tutu, resident of Mejguri. How many such unheard, unwritten and undelivered letters were sealed inside Sukurmani? As if she was a letter box posted as a milestone on an uneven footpath at some remote spot, withstanding the vagaries of seasons, sometimes soaked in rain, sometimes blotched in the scorching sun, but disfigured and discoloured the letter box stood erect in its place.

It is not that Sukurmani was always so stoical about the letter posted to her father. On the contrary, while dictating the letter that day, her eyes shone unusually bright. Hope and excitement made those jet black eyes seem bigger and shine brighter. She had noticed those eyes: they were beautiful and would look larger and smoky if kohl was applied to them. That day she had also noticed the shape of Sukurmani's face for the first time. She was dark no doubt, but there was a shine to her coppery black skin, a shine usually attained after a good oil massage. But leave aside a massage, she had no oil even for cooking. Her hair matched the colour of her skin and was jet black, shiny and silky. She had a broad forehead, bulky nose and lips and stood about four feet, ten inches tall. She wore her saree in her own distinctive style which was a blend of saree and the Assamese *mekhla*. How old must she be?

'What is your age, Sukurmani?' she had asked her.

'That I not know.'

'How old were you when you were married?'

'Then I very small, Memsaab.'

'Okay. Now you better tell me what I should be writing in the letter,' she said, trying to imitate her tone and diction.

'You write to him, Memsaab.' Those jet black, kohled eyes were lost somewhere in the lanes and by-lanes of her village Mejguri, searching for her father. An excess of missives, the inexplicable joy at this rare godsend opportunity of being able to send a letter to her father in this alien land imparted a juicy softness to her voice, as if someone had filled her mouth with jaggery. Saliva oozed from the corners of her mouth as she spoke.

'I send him money with our own man. Then for so many days I not send him money. So many days pass. Could not go back. No money. What are the sufferings and problems at your home? Write in your letter. Write, the child too is fine so long. In so many ways I meet father in my dreams. I always see him in my dreams. Don't know why I see him in my dreams in so many ways. It worries me. More than two years now passed. Two Durga Puja gone here. One here, the other in Kurichu. So many times I send him letter with our men. He replies if he got it. *Doonn't knowwee*.' The entire burden of Sukurmani's piled up anxieties and misgivings fell on those two words: 'Doonn't knowwee.'

'How can you be so sure that your father has not received your letter?'

'Memsaab, if he gets letter, he sends news.' There was just a touch of annoyance in her voice. 'Our men come here. I ask everybody. Doonn't knowwee where he goes,' she mumbled to herself.

'Okay. Tell me your father's name.' She took out the envelope to write the address on it.

'Sarju Tutu.'

But wasn't that also her son's name? 'Sukurmani, what is your son's name?' she asked to confirm.

'Surju.'

'Your father's name is Sarju Tutu. And your son's name is Surju Tutu.' Perhaps these people followed the matrilineal system whereby the son was given his maternal grandfather's name.

'Memsaab, I give my father's name to my child. Now that he has no father, how can I give him his father's name? If anything happen to us in this foreign land, where the child goes?' she explained.

Oblivious of the intricacies and complexities of native and foreign land, of life and death, the child's melodious voice could be heard reverberating through the air as he sang to himself. The boy was gifted with an enchanting voice. The vast expanse of the Brahmaputra, the fishermen rowing their boats on the river, casting their nets and singing to the tune of *hun-huna, hun-huna*—Surju's song was reminiscent of that mesmerising beauty of his native land.

'Is there a river in your village, Sukurmani?'

'Memsaab, my village has no river,' Sukurmani replied apologetically and somewhat perplexed. 'But yes, there is one small river if you cross Darranga. Do we also write river name in letter, Memsaab?' Her tone belied her confusion and a tinge of anxiety.

'No, no,' she smiled back. 'I was just curious to know. Now tell me the name of your village.'

'That post office is Parki Juli.'

'Shall I write Parki Juli as the name of your village?'

'That police post is Mela Bazar. All these things we people not know,' she replied in the same apologetic, somewhat perplexed voice.

'Okay. Just tell me, where does your father stay?'

'In Mejguri.'

Sarju Tutu,

Village Mejguri,

Post Office Parki Juli,

Police Station Mela Bazar,

Darranga.

She penned down the address in a neat hand in big, bold letters with a black ball pen.

'...Your daughter, Sukurmani. Done?'

'Memsaab, this is...' Sukurmani fumbled for words.

'Yes, what is it?'

'My name, Sukurmani, my father not know. He calls me Hujunmoi.'

Hujunmoi could be Sukurmani's pet name. She might have entered her name as Sukurmani in the labour register of GREF, the General Reserve Engineering Force, which works under the Border Roads Organisation (BRO).

'Here in *Greef* I work in my sister's name. First my sister works in Greef. Then I work in her name.'

'Where is your sister now?'

'She died. She had a child. The child is born, but after his birth my sister get *himsa*. She and her man worked there in Bishalgarh.'

'Where is her child now?'

'Dies before his mother. Dies after two days of birth.'

So her sister had died in childbirth.

'What about your sister's husband?'

'He is there in his village,' came the terse reply. Evidently, Sukurmani did not like her sister's husband very much.

'So how did you land up here in Kanglung?'

'When work finished there in our village, all people come here to work. No money there. Some people work in Bhutia's field, some people work in Greef. I also come here with people of our *des*.'

'How long did you work in GREF?' For someone so young, Sukurmani's itinerary was quite impressive. She looked barely in her early twenties.

'Memsaab, first we work in Bishalgarh. Surju's baba first works there. It was very good there. There we also make *raasi*. I make very good raasi, Memsaab. Here the Bhutias drink *arra*. There in India people say raasi.'

'Who taught you to brew raasi?' Like her itinerary, Sukurmani's job profile was equally impressive.

'Memsaab, in our village everyone make raasi. There everyone make very good raasi. It is not much cost. All you need is big pot and paddy. And what do you call that you give to Surju to eat that day?'

What had she given him? She tried in vain to recollect.

'That you eat with your mouth,' Sukurmani explained using her hands to demonstrate.

Now what is there that you don't eat with your mouth, Sukurmani! And then she got it—perhaps she had meant to say 'suck.' 'Do you mean sugarcane?'

'Yes, yes, that only. You boil it in raasi too.'

'What happened to Surju's baba?' More than the sugarcane, she wanted to know about Surju's father.

'Memsaab, he get *himsa*. We people not know in the beginning. In the beginning if we go to my baba, he cure it. Surju also then very small. He is taking my milk. I am not going out of house. I am very weak. What can his sister do? Surju's baba also not go out to work. We have no money. Then people of that des also trouble us. If there is money to give, no problem. I give raasi to *poolis* also. Oye baba! Those people fight so much with each other after they are taking raasi. Then that new *poolisman* comes and he very angry. He spill all our raasi! He take with him the pot too. Now we cannot make more raasi. If Surju's baba was there, we do not come here. That husband of my sister? Oye baba! He no good...!'

'Did Surju's baba sing?' she interrupted Sukurmani. More than her sister's husband, she wanted to know about Sukurmani's husband.

'Yes, Memsaab. How do you know?' she responded in wonder. Certainly Surju had inherited his singing skills from his father.

'Didn't you take Surju's baba to the hospital when he was sick?'

'Hospital very far, Memsaab. He cannot even get up from bed. He get too much *himsa*. We do not know in the beginning.'

This enigmatic, multi-dimensional, omnipresent *himsa* of Sukurmani she could never fathom until the very end. The root cause of all the troubles, conflicts, woes and sufferings in her life was this *himsa*; and the cure for it lay with her father. However, even he could not save Surju's baba for by then the *himsa* had gone beyond cure.

'So should I now call you Hujunmoi?' She could empathise with the dilemma of being known and addressed by someone else's name, and felt she must restore her name and identity.

Sukurmani was silent for some time. Then she said, 'Here everybody call me Sukurmani. It has been for too long.'

It was true. She, too, had got used to calling her Sukurmani.

Troubled and anxious about her father's wellbeing, working in an alien land with the borrowed identity of her dead sister and giving her fatherless son the shelter of her own father's name, Sukumani would unfailingly come to work in her house every morning.

The eagerly awaited response to the letter dispatched to Sukurmani's father did not come. But in the post-letter phase, a distinct change was evident in Sukurmani's behaviour. She would smile at her now and then, make small talk about something or the other, or enquire about her wellbeing. 'Is it holiday today, Memsaab?' she would ask, or 'Today you go late?' Sometimes she would sweep the backyard on her own and burn the debris and fallen leaves. There was no sweeper assigned for such odd jobs; the Drukpas themselves did them. Sometimes Sukurmani would water the plants, or fetch vegetables and groceries from the shop in the upper market. Occasionally, she would pick up the oil bottle and give her a head massage. If you didn't ask her to stop, the massage could continue for hours. That day when Sukurmani began to gently pull at her hair, fixing the strands adroitly in-between her fingers, she asked her, 'Where did you pick this up? You are an expert at this!'

much *himsa* to us. So I come here with Surju. If I take Surju there with me, Memsaab, there is *himsa* for Surju.'

It was the month of March. The bare, dry branches of trees were now laden with white, pink and yellow flowers. The east-Bhutanese dialect of Sharchopa had unobtrusively mingled with Surju's speech like the sweet spring air. Little Surju's routine was inseparable from that of his mother. Get up from bed and follow in her footsteps; mother in front and behind her the calf following her trail. If he found a piece of tin or anything of the kind on the way, he would pick it up. Sometimes Sukurmani would make a hole in the lid of an empty boot-polish tin and fix it with a cord, which he would trail on the ground to a tinny rhythmic rattle as he walked behind her, and that gave him more joy than all the toys in the world possibly could give. The open grounds facing her bungalow were full of all kinds of trees, shrubs, flowers, dried cones, twigs and leaves to entice the fancy of an imaginative child. At times the boy was entranced by the deodar cones lying in thick profusion on the ground; at times the official vehicles parked in the compound would draw his unwavering attention. Since this was a government bungalow, there were a number of preambles earmarked for Surju: he must not pluck the flowers and the grass on the lawn, must not touch any of the vehicles parked there or clamber on top of them. All these restrictions had been imposed on him only after he had tried his hand at these tabooed activities.

But how long can you restrain a restless four-year old? His mother would be busy in the kitchen, and every once in a while Surju would give her the slip. She would constantly have to devise ways in which to keep him busy. Had he been in his own country, he would be in some government school. How long could he loiter around aimlessly, forever trailing behind his mother? But as per the rules of this country, he was neither of the age for admission to school nor could he seek admission here under any circumstances. Here, one year was added to a child's age at the time of birth to account for the time it is inside the mother's womb. According to this logic, a child's admissible age for school was six years. There was only one primary school in the town of Kanglung where the tuition fee was waived and the cost of books, stationery and all educational expenses were borne by the state. Understandably, the children of the state had the first rightful claim to enjoy the state's welfare benefits. So the Indians had to virtually run from pillar to post to admit their wards in the primary school. After all, what was the need for the children of migrant Indian labourers to go to school and be educated! It was far more beneficial for their parents, and for the children when they grew up, if they worked as household help. But Sukurmani was confident that Surju would be admitted to school.

'I send him to school. He is small. Next year Surju goes to school.'

What can an idle child do for hours? To engage him, she gave Surju a copy and pencil. She also wished to buy books for him, but there was no bookshop in the market. Initially, she tried to teach him the Hindi alphabet, but she soon grew disillusioned as it seemed a futile exercise. For neither here in Kanglung nor there in Darranga or in Mejguri in India were these Hindi alphabets going to be of much use to Surju. And once he returned to Mejguri, how useful even English would be to him was anyone's guess.

'He calls you amma?' she asked Sukurmani.

'Yes. This is how he calls me.'

'Do they say amma in your parts too?'

'No. There they say that.... In Rungthung the children say amma, so he pick it up from them.'

Between the mother and son whether the two conversed in Bodo or Dumka dialect, she did not know. As for herself she finally, albeit reluctantly, settled for English, the global language to be taught to Surju. After all, Surju too was a citizen of the world, transcending the geographical boundaries of India, Bangladesh,

Bhutan, Assam or Bodoland; he did not need the citizenship of any country. Today he is in Bhutan. Who knows he might make his way to Nepal tomorrow via Phuntoshiling. Or if he caught a fancy for the gravel pathway down below the main tarred road in Deothang in Bhutan, Surju may one day enlist himself in the secret forces of the Bodos or the ULFA who had their camps in these forests; one did not need a work permit for these kinds of jobs. Over and above, whether you trespass into the forests of Deothang or the town of Kanglung, hunger is by far the strongest driving force. If Surju were to become a labourer working on border roads and bridges like his mother, he need not know any particular language for it. Tomorrow, some Drukpa, much in the manner of Dorji Pinjor, one of her students, would write down panegyrics for these Indian labourers in his composition:

'They gave their today for our tomorrow. When we walk these roads, drive past them, we should not forget that some Indian's sweat is immersed in them.' But how many of the Drukpas thought the same was anyone's guess.

As for the present, little Surju master was busy drawing quietly on paper with a pencil—a welcome respite from the screeching music produced by the interplay of the tin lids of polish and the jarring staccato of his oversized plastic gumboots. Unfortunately, this drawing programme did not last long. One day she noticed to her dismay the pristine, recently painted walls of the porch decorated with Surju's sprawling horizontal and vertical line drawings. Apparently, the ingenious budding artist had used the walls as his canvas.

'Surju, don't you bring your pencil here from tomorrow! You better try these drawings at your home,' she told him angrily.

Once again Surju was free to loiter around in the lawn. The bamboo grove in the backyard of her bungalow was the abode of birds whose chirping resounded in the air mornings and evenings. Tiny black crows, which the Drukpa called *chungas,* red-beaked sparrows, parrots, pigeons, cuckoos, black and brown nightingales, thrushes and a variety of other colourful birds were a usual sight, perched on the branches of trees or hopping about on the ground among the flowers. There was a bird-watching club in town and the young college boys could be seen in the early morning hours with their binoculars. More than half of Surju's time was spent watching these birds as they took off to the sky when he chased them from the bushes or in scattering leftovers for them. Sometimes he would call out excitedly for his mother.

'What does he say?' She was curious to know.

'Memsaab, he tells me to come out. There is a nice bird, he wants me to see it,' Sukurmani said, her face lighting up with a smile all the more brightly at the interest shown by her Memsaab.

Once in a while, Surju had the company of the Drukpa boy while Sukurmani was busy at work. Her Drukpa neighbour's son, the boy was also an only child like Surju and needed a playmate. But after just three or four days of camaraderie and frolic, the two would invariably drift apart. There was no match between Surju in his grubby, soiled clothes, incessantly wiping his runny nose on his sleeve and dragging his oversized plastic shoes, and the healthy, well-groomed, fair Drukpa boy. Be it Bhutan or India, native or foreign land, the well-off and the wealthy all around the globe belong to one clan, one caste, one fraternity.

Notwithstanding these social divisions and dualities, Surju's life progressed at a relatively even pace in his own world marked by empty polish tins, matchboxes, cigarette cases, picture cuttings from newspapers and magazines, wooden carts and deodar cones, watching the dazzling array of birds in the shrubs, on trees and in the open skies of Kanglung, befriending the stray dogs on the streets, and intently watching the Drukpa children going to school. He could hear his mother's call of 'Oye baba!' from any corner of the compound. His appreciative, musical expression of 'Oho!' at the sight of breakfast, the intimate tete-a-tete of mother and son sharing the meal, and the sweetness of all the sweetmeats in Sukurmani's voice—a mother's profound joy in being able to provide breakfast for her child. These were the simple joys of their life.

Once in a while she, too, joined in their repartees, especially on holidays when she was in no hurry to go to work.

That day for the first time she heard Sukurmani's loud, uninhibited laughter in response to some remark made by her son.

'What does he say?'

'Memsaab, he tells me to hurry and come fast or he eat up everything,' Sukurmani replied, her eyes twinkling.

Be it the sharing of breakfast or getting up from bed in the wee hours of the morning or the breaking of stones on the roadside—in all tasks big and small, in joy and in sorrow, in all ups and downs of this journey called life, the mother and son were equal partners.

Often, more than half of Sukurmani's conversation was beyond her comprehension. If she understood what Sukurmani said she would reply in monosyllables, yes or no as the case may be, or else manage with a noncommittal nod. But that day, Sukurmani was bent upon making her point clear and understood. She squatted down before her on the floor with the tray of vegetables and began to chop them as she talked.

'Memsaab, that letter does not come.'

She was worried about Sukurmani's father, but more for Sukurmani. There was every possibility that he could have met with some casualty during this interval; otherwise he would surely have responded to the letter. Darranga was about a hundred and fifty or two hundred kilometres at the most from this place. The Indian Army's Dantak unit was in Darranga as well as in Kanglung, and the postal services between these two important army stations operated on a regular basis. She had dispatched Sukurmani's letter along with Dantak's official post. But then, who was there back home to be really interested in Sukurmani's whereabouts? Had she not travelled all the way from her village to this foreign land only to escape the *himsa* of those 'near and dear ones?'

'Is your mother alive?' she asked, but she already knew the answer. Sukurmani would have surely referred to her if she were alive.

'Mother dies when I am there. There is *aik thu* father.' Having worked with the Bihari and Nepali labourers for long, Sukurmani had acquired some of their typical linguistic expressions and nuances. *Aik thu,* meaning only or only the one, was very commonly used by the Nepalis and added to almost every second sentence they spoke: aik thu house, aik thu road. 'Mother dies there,' Sukurmani repeated. Who knows; perhaps she, too, lost her life in the maramari, the internal feuds of the Kukis and Dumkas.

'I am here for two Durga Puja. In the previous Durga Puja, I am in Kurichu. There you do not know if it is Durga Puja. I should be getting his news if he is alive.' The speed at which Sukurmani's fingers were chopping the vegetables seemed to slacken a little with the lowering of her voice. 'Memsaab, I could go if there is *peesa*.'

Trust a daughter's psyche! Just the other day, in response to her suggestion of paying for the journey home, Sukurmani had ruled out the possibility of going back to her village on the grounds that she might face problems in returning to Kanglung. But when the tide of emotions runs high, the economics of profit and loss and all other considerations take a back seat. Over the persistent chirping and chatter of other birds, one could now hear the loud crowing of the chungas, the small Bhutani crows. The crowing of this bird was considered to be the forerunner of news, mostly the arrival of a guest. Perhaps right now they were conveying a father's message to his daughter in this distant land.

'So you were in Kurichu before you came to Kanglung?'

'Yes, Memsaab. I work first in Kurichu. Then I work in Rungthung. There he *distubs* us a lot. He does not let the child sleep at night. Spends all my peesa. Drinks raasi with my peesa.'

'Who was he?'

'That *ssala* Bihari! He tell me nicely, you are single, I also single, so let us live together. I can have proper food, you and Surju too can have proper food; so I go stay with him. In the beginning Memsaab, he come home in good way, not taking raasi too. He talk to Surju in nice way. But then he take raasi, Memsaab. Does not give me peesa.

Take away all my peesa also and say many many bad things about me everywhere. Oye baba! So I leave Rungthung and come here. How can we stay there? Otherwise I wouldn't be here, Memsaab.' From the regret in her voice, it was evident that Sukurmani had been happy in Rungthung.

One voice, endless complaints. How was this lone, solitary voice to bear the brunt of all these countless complaints, misgivings and troubles? Where would the water on the river banks drift and diverge if not on the sandy grounds?

'Ssala! That rogue tells our men, he will break my bones if he see me in Rungthung!'

'How dare he talk like that?' A fine instance of bullying this was! 'Whether you want to stay with him or not is entirely your decision. How can he impose himself on you? You should have informed your employer about him. You lost your job. So who was the ultimate loser—he or you? He is having a gala time there. It is only you who has been forced to drift from one place to another with Surju.' But that Bihari fellow was also deprived of free access to wine and woman.

'Oh Memsaab, I go a bit late to my Saab one day. So he go to my Saab early morning and *repot* that I run away with his things and money! See Memsaab, where can I hide his things?'

It was true. With no roof over her head, what could this small woman of four feet, nine inches possibly lift in her arms—her son, or this Bihari partner's belongings?

Her eyes fixed on the ground, Sukurmani's fingers were chopping vegetables with a knife at an even pace. If these hands were busy working the spade in Rungthung, she would be earning fifty rupees a day. The other day Sukurmani had shared this information with her that the daily wage for the GREF labourers had been hiked up to fifty rupees. In addition, they were entitled to leave on Sundays and other holidays.

'Memsaab, I could work if I get work here.' Sometimes, Sukurmani's abrupt responses and comments were like pearls scattered from a necklace; it was left to the listener to string them together and give them shape and meaning. Now who was to employ Sukurmani here in Kanglung, and how?

'Last night that man not let us sleep, Memsaab. The boy also cries. I cannot get up in time in the morning. That Bhutia too is angry with me. He tell me: Go, find some other room.'

So this was the crux of the matter. 'Who is that man?' she asked.

'That man, Memsaab, who is from our des. He is the one who give us this room to stay. He is very nice to us in the day, will not talk to us. But every day at night he *distub* us. The child too is so...'

'So are you staying here with this man now?' she interrupted Sukurmani, annoyance creeping into her voice.

'No, no, Memsaab,' Sukurmani contradicted her emphatically. 'We stay in our room. His wife is with him. He has children too. The girl who come other day with Surju...?' Yes, she remembered; a girl of Surju's age had accompanied them to her house one day. 'She is his daughter. He too have son. He is there in Rungthung with us. I tell him when your wife is with you, why do you *distub* us?'

'You should have spoken frankly to his wife.'

'Yes, Memsaab, I speak *frunkly* to his wife. But if she say anything to him, he beat her and abuse her too.'

So what was the solution to this? Unlike in the fable, here the two cats were not quarrelsome; even then the monkey had his day.

'In the day he is nice to us, Memsaab. Very nice. Will not talk to us or even look at us. Sometimes he plays with the child. Only at night he *distubs* us. Oye baba! Bangs door so loudly! Door cannot be bolted from inside. No bolt. The child also cries.'

Having forgotten all the woes of the troublesome night, the boy was happily beating the two lids of the polish tin to his own rhythm and lustily singing.

Pardesi, pardesi jana nahin, hamein chhor kar
O foreigner from a foreign land, don't you go leaving us behind

Now Surju had many Hindi songs in his kitty as well.

She looked at the watch. It was nine o'clock, and she had not had her breakfast yet. Early in the morning this woman had come up with this senseless narrative.

'How can every Tom, Dick and Harry disturb you whenever he so desires?' she said in an irate, high-pitched voice. 'In Rungthung the Bihari disturbs you. Here someone of your own country disturbs you.' You are not such a beauty that all the men in Kanglung and Rungthung should be after you, she muttered under her breath.

'Memsaab, he *distub* us only when he drink raasi,' Sukurmani tried to bring home her point. The real culprit was liquor, not the man.

'So what is there to be afraid of if he is drunk? There is no reason to be scared of a drunkard. Just get hold of a stick and hit it hard on his head! He will collapse there and then.'

'Memsaab, yesterday I scold him. I say so many things to him in front of his wife. Just see, Memsaab, now his wife also tells me to leave the room.'

'Forget it. Let her say whatever she wants. You don't vacate the room. If you are intimidated by people, people will always intimidate you. If you had to be bullied by all the men here, you should have stayed back in your own country. Why did you come here?' She was getting a little exasperated by these frequent instances of harassment that to her reflected to a certain extent the lack of willpower on Sukurmani's part. This woman needs to hold her ground, or else she will just be swept off by this horde of ruffians.

Unfazed by her sarcasm, Sukurmani replied with her usual calm, 'First I go to my des, Memsaab. When Surju's baba dies, I cannot go to his brother's house. Oye baba! There that brother of Surju's baba and his wife do so much *himsa* to us. Surju's baba and I work in the field whole day. Then I work at home also. They do not give us enough food to eat. Do *himsa* to us too. Then Surju's baba say to me, "When these people do *himsa* to us and do not give us full meal, we shall go and work at some other place." Then we leave the village and go to Bishalgarh. It was very good there in Bishalgarh. If only Surju's baba had not suffered from *himsa*. He very good, does not take raasi, does not beat me. Never. Speaks nicely to me. That husband of my sister! Oye baba! He does not give food to my sister. He drink raasi too. If Surju's baba was not dead, I would not be here, Memsaab.'

'Then why didn't you go to your baba's village?'

'I go there, Memsaab. I go there with Surju and his sister. There my brother and his wife do so much *himsa* to me. My brother also drinks raasi. Surju's sister dies there of *himsa*. I too had *himsa*, but my father knows about it in time and cures me.'

So Surju also had an elder sister. She sneaked a glance into Sukurmani's eyes: those eyes were tearless, there was no moisture there. She narrated the bygones in so detached and dispassionate a manner as if the narrative belonged to someone else, not her.

'Did Surju have an elder sister, too?'

'Yes, Memsaab. If she alive today, she would be my height. There would be no problem then. She could take care of her brother Surju at home. She would be as tall as me.'

The young daughter of a widowed mother—who can say if she would have been a support, or another excuse for further disturbance at odd hours from Biharis and other fellow countrymen.

'There was no problem if Surju's sister was there with me.' The needle of Sukurmani's narrative was now stuck on Surju's sister. If only she were alive today, Sukurmani would have had someone to look to. Surju's sister would have brought all her mother's miseries to an end.

Perhaps for a few days Sukurmani was not bothered by her fellow countryman as there was no further reference to him.

'It seems that these days your neighbour, that fellow of your des, doesn't disturb you?'

'He not here, Memsaab. He go to India with family. His wife is expecting child.'

Poor Sukurmani. How long could a he-goat's mother remain carefree? Sooner or later, the goat has to be butchered. Once the man returned leaving his family behind, he would be in a much more convenient position to disturb Sukurmani as and when he so desired. And anyway, his wife's presence hardly mattered.

Given their circumstances and harsh living conditions, these labourers were also not entirely to be blamed. Working on roadsides and living in labour camps, they could hardly afford to keep their families with them. The men could manage with the makeshift roadside huts and camps, but to keep their families with them they needed a better social support system. Their physical needs had to be fulfilled and in the absence of their wives, co-women workers like Sukurmani became the soft targets.

'Listen, you need not be scared of him when he comes back. Let me make it very clear to you, Sukurmani: no one dare disturb you in the middle of the night if you are not interested. All that is required is strength of character and some kind of reserve on the part of a woman. I, too, am staying alone. No one disturbs me.' She added the last sentence after a second thought. She would not like to compare herself with Sukurmani, but this woman should know how to carry herself.

Suddenly, she was overwhelmed by a desire to help this illiterate fellow country sister, struggling singlehandedly in this foreign land with a small child for the sake of a little money. Just a few words of sympathy and a patient hearing were sufficient to impart moral and spiritual strength to Sukurmani, she felt. Until then, she believed so.

There was an acute shortage of maidservants in the Indian expatriate colony. The practice of working as housemaids was not popular among the Drukpa womenfolk who preferred to work on their own farmlands, grow vegetables, weave fine cloth on handlooms, while the lazier ones were content to be at home and get drunk on arra. The ghos and kiras worn by them were handwoven, and so were the carpets in their homes. A small number of Drukpa and Lhotshampa, the southern Bhutani women of Nepali origin, worked as maids for Canadian and Australian expatriate families and were well paid. For the Indian housewives, accustomed to enjoying the services of maids back home for negligible sums, the very idea of paying two thousand rupees a month to a maid was unpalatable. And these middle-class Indian housewives were not used to doing domestic work—none of them would be cleaning utensils and mopping floors back home in India.

'Who works at your house?' This would be the preamble for any kind of conversation among the Indian housewives at parties or similar social functions. These parties were practically the only occasions that offered them a welcome respite from their everyday monotonous routines.

'Left with no one! I'm doing all the household chores myself.' It was Mrs. Venkatraman.

'Why? There was a girl who used to work at your house. I forget now, what was her name?' The ever curious Mrs. Singh turned to Mrs. Venkatraman.

'Norbo. It is by no means easy to get work done by these girls. Her brother used to accompany her everyday. Then one day she said her brother wasn't well, so how could she travel all the way from Rungthung by herself?' Mrs. Venkatraman replied, throwing a sly sideways glance at her.

And then she would be the ultimate target of all these direct and indirect hints, insinuations and sideways glances of these gossipmongers since she was the only notable exception in their colony who enjoyed the luxury of a regular maid, and that too a good one.

'What's the name of that woman ...? Yes, I recollect. Sukurmani. She has grabbed work in most of the households. How can these poor young girls travel all the way from Rungthung to Kanglung to work in just one or two houses? The track is no doubt very lonely and unsafe, especially for girls. Then there is also the danger of wild animals.'

'You know last week I had visited the Dantak labour camp. There are hardly two or three labourers' families residing there. The women in the camp easily find work in the officers' quarters.

Moreover, they prefer to be hired as labourers on construction sites; in fact most of them are working on construction sites,' Mrs. Venkatraman was telling the others. She was right. Given a choice, even Sukurmani would have preferred to be hired by GREF.

'They are better paid as labourers,' she hit back with a pinch of salt in her voice. If there really was such a crisis for domestic help as they all professed, why not be a little more generous with payments like their Canadian and Australian counterparts?

'Yes, at GREF they also get leave on Sundays,' rejoined Mrs. Rai, half supporting her. 'I had such a tough time with my maid. She would always give me the slip on Sundays!'

Though she understood every bit of their guarded and not-so-guarded gossip, she nevertheless pretended to be naive and refused to take the bait. Desperate for a maid, the housewives invariably turned to her for help.

'Please do talk to your maid and ask her if she would work for me. She comes to your house in the morning. She could come to me anytime during the day since I am at home. She can come to me after finishing work at your place. You won't be affected at all, I promise you,' Mrs. Rao pleaded.

'You better talk to Sukurmani yourself, Mrs. Rao,' she replied evasively. She had no interest in meddling in these useless and time-consuming affairs.

'I have talked to her, but she did not give me a final answer and said she would talk to you first.' Now that Sukurmani had reposed such faith in the judgement of her Memsaab, she was obliged to honour that trust.

'Memsaab, that Nandu, you know him, he asks me to work for him,' Sukurmani said to her without preliminaries one day.

'Who is Nandu?'

'Who lives in building below the road. His son comes here that day, plays with Surju.'

'*Nandu*! Sukurmani, you are impossible! You call him Nandu as if he were some school-going boy. His name is Dr. Rao. He teaches in the college.' Dr. Rao would not be amused if he came to know of this honorific. Apparently Sukurmani had not been too impressed by the impeccably dressed Dr. Rao who never ventured out of his house without a tie on his suit. 'Who told you about this name of Dr. Rao?' she asked, trying her best to suppress her laughter.

'This is how his wife calls him, Memsaab. That day we meet them in the upper market. They ask me to carry their bags home. There are too many bags. He gives me five-*thu* rupees too. Then his wife calls him Nandu. That other name we people do not know, Memsaab,' she replied apologetically.

'Never mind. How much are they going to pay you?'

'That I not ask them.'

'Then you better ask. You should work for them only if they pay you at least one thousand and five hundred rupees a month. There are quite a few other families you could work for.'

'Memsaab, what is... his name who asks me to work for them?'

'Dr. Rao.'

'Yes, *Dacter* Rao. That Dacter Rao's wife asks me how much peesa your Memsaab gives you. I tell her my Memsaab gives me sixteen hundred-*thu* rupee. There is not much work also. Single person. How much work can be? Not many utensils to clean. She give breakfast too. Nobody can give this much.'

'Why did you say that?' She knew it forbode trouble for her. That day when Babu Moshai had walked past her on way to the upper market without acknowledging her, she knew he was displeased with her for some reason. Later she heard from Sukurmani that his maid had demanded a hike. A stingy man who may well part with his skin but not his money, Babu Moshai was a seasoned shopper who wouldn't buy even a pin without a thorough scrutiny of the whole lot. The day he visited the army canteen, half the items would go into his kitty. Now who was to question him about what he wanted to do with twelve bottles of honey. Had he spared a few bottles, they could have been of some use to other families as well, especially those with small children, in minor ailments like cough and cold. You must have a maid, must enjoy all the facilities and amenities of life, but with the minimum amount of expenditure.

She was quite often piqued by this mindset of the Indian expatriates in Bhutan. Their miserliness reflected in their manners and their behaviour, in the upkeep of their houses and in their private as well as public dealings. They were here to earn money; everything else was immaterial to them. More than an individual, an expatriate in a foreign country is a representative of his nation. If not for themselves, at least for the sake of the prestige and goodwill of their country if only these people could behave in a more dignified manner. No wonder the Indians never earned the same respect from the locals as their European and Canadian counterparts.

But expatriates like Babu Moshai are not entirely to be blamed for such a mindset and social apathy. It is not easy to spend year in, year out in complete isolation in a remote corner of the world where one is literally cut off from the outside world with little or no access even to basic, everyday necessities of life. If you need to travel, there is no means of transport; if someone is sick at your house, there is no doctor in the vicinity; if you wish to buy grocery, there is no market and if there is a market there are no shops; if there are shops there are no goods available in them, and if there are goods available occasionally, there are no means of transportation to carry them home. If there is one vehicle, there would be fifty people in line to board it. You could walk around the whole town in less than an hour, coming across the same familiar faces each and every day. You would crave for some tiny titbits and your pockets may be full of notes, but the shops are empty. Once in a while the vegetable supplies would reach the shops, and people would virtually jump on them like a pack of hungry dogs and crows. In such a situation, why won't someone hoard twelve bottles of honey, or quietly avail a lift in some private, city-bound vehicle and sneak out? As the saying goes, one pomegranate, a hundred sick. Confined for years in such a habitat, one's perspective and priorities do get influenced and limited to one's personal and familial interests.

Eventually, the Rao family employed Sukurmani for a monthly wage of one thousand and four hundred rupees. She seemed quite content with her new job; it was evident from the spring in her step.

'Where is Surju?' she asked Sukurmani one day when he had not accompanied his mother. Was her neighbour back? Had she left the child with his family? Was this newfound joy and peace of Sukurmani so shortlived then?

'He plays with Sanju, Memsaab,' she replied with a smile, a mother's pride and joy writ large on her radiant face. Rao's son Sanju was also the only child and thus deprived of a playmate. His second-hand clothes had done wonders for Surju, whose small person had undergone a pleasant transformation of sorts. Otherwise his curly brown matted hair, his pants smeared with dried mud, the variegated patches of dirt on his faded filthy coat and the oversize plastic gumboots to top it all—these had become his trademarks, identifiable from a distance. His nose was perpetually leaking and the moment her eyes would meet his, he would begin to rub his nose on his sleeve in nervousness.

'Sukurmani, blow his nose. Why don't you give him a piece of cloth to wipe his nose?' she would often say in exasperation. Sometimes she would herself give him a handkerchief or a piece of clean cloth, but the mother-son duo circumambulating the town of Kanglung umpteen times a day might drop it anywhere on the way. Oh those big, round eyes of his! Whenever she made eye contact with Surju, she experienced something intense, peculiar and inexplicable. Was it love? A little perhaps. Or was it more anxiety? It was certainly a strange feeling of unease. To some extent, even dread. She could never squarely confront those dark black eyes for more than half a minute. But at times she had an overwhelming desire to hug Surju, to caress or fondle him, to talk to him.

Whenever he spoke to his mother she would observe there was a distinct change in his tone; he would sound all grown up, like a man. After all, wasn't he his mother's sole guardian? The Hindu prayer: *Tumhi ho mata, pita tumhi ho, tumhi ho bandhu, sakha tumhi ho,* You are the mother, You are the father, You only are the friend and companion, applied perfectly to this duo. For the one complemented the other—they were indispensible to each other. A few months later, she would witness Surju in the role of a responsible guardian—the guardian of his mother and sister.

That day a vehicle was heading towards Kurichu. Work was in progress on a hydro power plant run by the Government of India. Power was supplied to the town of Kanglung from the Rungthung power station. In Dzongkha and Sharchopa, *chhu* means water. Whether it was a river, spring, lake or just water, chhu sufficed. If a river passed through a town, the suffix of chhu was added to the name of that town and a new river was conveniently named. For instance, Kurichhu or Kurichi river, Hachhu or Ha river, Parochhu or Paro river and so on. The bridge on the river Kurichhu was under construction. The next step would be the generation of power. Once the power plant was completed, in the surrounding hills and valleys, for ages enveloped in the darkness of night, thousands of fireflies would glow. Sukurmani and many of her fellow sisters and brothers would be the behind-the-scene actors to this luminous glory of the night. Sooner or later all of them would head back to their homelands. Would Sukurmani, too, be able to make it to her des? But to which homeland would she return: Darranga? Dumka? Ranchi? Bihar? Or would she prefer to stay back in Bhutan? Only the future held the key to all these questions.

That memorable journey from Kanglung to Kurichu! That unforgettable thirty-kilometre long stretch! After crossing the town of Trashigang in eastern Bhutan, which is twenty-five kilometres from Kanglung, there is no sign of any human habitation, not a roadside shop or petrol pump in sight. Far ahead on your right and left you confront nothing but the high overarching solid, rocky mountains. Flowing in the opposite direction along the road is a solitary river. Transfixed on the roadside, the massive age-old boulders. Passing through the foothills this river runs from Arunachal Pradesh in India. From the hills of Arunachal Pradesh the river flows down the eastern and central region of Bhutan, finally converging with the waters of the Brahmaputra in India. In the course of its long journey via Bhutan, the river is adorned with many names. In Wangdecholing, which is famous for its lake, the wintering ground for the black-necked cranes, it is called Wangdecholingchhu. Moving downwards, the lake water mingles with the river in the town of Trashiyangtsi where it acquires a new name—Kholingchhu. Thus, in Kurichu the river is called Kurichuchhu, and in Trashigang where it converges with Tawangchhu, as Dangmechhu.

Parallel to this river runs a solitary road whose silence is only occasionally disturbed by a passing vehicle or army truck. Working on the bridge construction site one can see Indian labourers and their huts lined up on the roadside. Otherwise, there is not a speck of civilization or development to mar the silence of nature here; those labourers are the only representatives of human life in this wilderness. Sukurmani too had taken part in the construction of this bridge; she too had broken stones for the walls of the bridge. The occupant of one of these huts was a Bihari who had said to Sukurmani, 'You are single, so am I. Let us be together.'

She could instantly fathom the significance of the term 'single.' Sukurmani's account of her sojourn in Kurichu would have been incomprehensible without firsthand encountering this visual, geographical context—seeing *is* believing. This singularity or solitary status of the Bihari labourer did not imply the singularity implicit in Tagore's song: *Aikla chalo re, jodi tor daak shune keo na aashe tobey aikla chalo re*, walk alone, if no one comes when you call, walk alone. Neither was it the goal of worldly renunciation that the ancient sages had spoken of. Implicit in this solitary existence was the collective chant of these labourers toiling hard to fill so many empty stomachs back home and the silent chants of their families anxiously waiting for money orders. This intriguing phenomenon belied the oft-quoted maxim of seasoned loners: *Aikantvasa, na jhagra na jhasa*, a solitary life, no quarrels, no intrigues. These simple labourers coped with such stark, unendurable loneliness without any philosophical or spiritual anchor.

And then out of the blue that teenaged girl had materialised from somewhere and quietly stood by her side.

'Your name is Norbo, isn't it?' she asked her with a smile. She was so pleased to see a familiar human face in this wilderness.

The girl nodded in affirmation.

'Do you stay here?'

Yes, she answered with a nod.

'Were you in Rungthung sometime back?'

There was again the affirming nod.

'Who else is there in your family?'

'Baba and my sister. There is my baba,' the girl spoke up at last, pointing her finger towards a labourer at the construction site. Her language was the usual mix of Nepali and Bihari.

'Are you Nepali?'

'No,' came the answer with a forceful shake of the head. 'I am Drukpa.'

'Sukurmani also used to work in Rungthung, didn't she?' She tried to change the topic from ethnicity to a common, safe ground.

'Yes. She works for you now, isn't it?' Norbo's flat tone reflected a spark of interest. 'I can also work for you if she doesn't.' Norbo had been employed by Mrs. Mehta until last month.

'Yes. Sukurmani works for me. Do you know her?'

'Yes. She was also in Rungthung when we were there.'

She avoided looking at the girl; both her hands and feet were full of specks and moles. Meanwhile, another girl of Norbo's age had joined them. She must not be more than eleven or twelve. Very lean and thin. Distinctly Indian features. Better not ask. In these parts, it was so difficult to distinguish between Indians, Bangladeshis and the southern Bhutanese and Drukpas.

'Were you in Kanglung sometime back?' she asked this newcomer; her face also seemed familiar. The girl was staring straight at her with those deep black eyes. But unlike Norbo she was not at all shy.

'Yes, of course,' shot back the reply. 'Don't you remember? I worked in your friend's house.'

Yes, she could recollect now. This girl used to work for her colleague Sudha Saxsena.

'Why did you stop working for my friend?' Sudha Saxsena had been on the lookout for a maid for a long time after this girl disappeared one day and did not show up again. Now Sukurmani worked in her house.

'My mother is here in Kurichu now. She does not allow me to go to Kanglung. That is why.'

'Does your mother work here then?'

She nodded a yes.

'Does your father also work here?'

'No.' The glow on her face instantly faded.

'She has no father,' said Norbo, quickly coming to her rescue.

'She has no mother,' the girl responded, levelling the score with Norbo. This is how it was. All the vehicles had one or the other wheel missing, somewhere the front wheel, elsewhere the back one. Where all the wheels were intact, the main body would be missing or broken. Nonetheless, the vehicle of life moved on, even if not speedily or steadily. It is these people with fractured families and broken human ties who were building the dams and bridges on rivers; sometimes they acted as the bridges between two nations, sometimes as the roads on which trucks and lorries carried goods from this side of the border to the other. As for the road, it always remained silent, never budging an inch from its place.

'What is your name?' she asked the other girl.

'Pratima.'

Judging from her accent, she could be from Bangladesh. 'Where are you from?'

'India,' came the emphatic reply.

Here, in this remote corner of the world, they were all Indians, citizens of the erstwhile undivided Indian subcontinent who did not require any proof of identity.

'Sukurmani, yesterday I had gone to Kurichu. I also passed through your Rungthung,' she told Sukurmani when she came in for work the next morning.

'You go *there*, Memsaab?' Sukurmani responded, the eagerness evident in her voice.

'Yes, I went to see the dam under construction. Didn't you work in Kurichu before coming here?'

'Yes, I work there too. Other people who work with me are still there.' There was a tinge of sadness in her voice.

'How did you cook food there?' She hadn't seen any shop, any patches of farmland or any sign of human habitation apart from the labourers at the construction site. Only those huge boulders and rocks for miles together.

'Ration comes from Darranga, Memsaab. In truck. The day meals are cooked in camp.'

'Who cooks food for all the people?'

'We people only. Those of us who are given *dooty* cook food. Then for night we get ration. We also get *ghaslet* there.' The nostalgic note in her emphatic 'ghaslet,' local parlance for kerosene, was all too evident.

'Is kerosene easily available here in Kanglung?' Sukurmani must be cooking food on the kerosene stove.

'No, Memsaab. Here in shops, what you call it, *keroseen*, we do not get it any time,' she bemoaned.

'Then how do you cook food?' Till date Sukurmani had never mentioned that this was a problem.

'I collect firewood and cook food with that. Surju also bring firewood. Sometimes that Bhutia give me ghaslet.'

It suddenly dawned on her—this woman never asked for anything. Everyday, Sukurmani moved the five-litre canny full of kerosene, kept in the corner of her kitchen, from its place while mopping the floor, and then put it back where it was without ever uttering a word about it.

'Why didn't you tell me that you needed kerosene oil? There is some in the canny. You can take it,' she told her, feeling guilty.

'But you also need it for making fire, no. Memsaab, do you go to Rungthung also?' Just then, the update on her former co-workers was clearly of greater interest to her than kerosene.

'Yes, I also visited Rungthung. I met that girl Norbo. Isn't she a Nepali?' The girl spoke Hindi with a Nepali accent.

'Her mother was Nepali.'

'Where is her mother now? I hope she is alive.'

'Yes, alive. She go to India with another man. Leave behind Norbo with her elder sister Pema. Her elder sister very good. She do household work also. This Norbo not help her sister in household work. Always say bad thing to her father.'

'Wasn't Norbo working here in Kanglung sometime back?'

'This Norbo will not work in one place. Not listen to her father and sister. Not give her peesa to anybody.'

She recalled how Norbo's face had fallen at the mention of her father. Poor girl! On whom would she vent her anger and frustration if not on those closest to her? If the father were also to follow in his wife's footsteps, the girl would be left with no one to call her own.

'There was another girl with Norbo. Pratima. Is she a Bangladeshi?'

'No, Memsaab, they are from Kokrajhar. This Pratima's father was killed there in maramari. Now Pratima's mother has only aik thu daughter. I do not know why this Pratima's mother is like that.' The pitch of Sukurmani's voice abruptly grew shrill. 'She never talk to anyone. Never smile at anyone. She not let Pratima speak with anyone. Sometimes Pratima come to play with Surju. But her mother come there and take her away, is angry with her. You should speak nicely to people.'

Sukurmani, you spoke nicely to all and sundry, but how did it help you? Perhaps she had never heard the adage: *hansi to phansi*—if a woman smiles, she's as good as snared. After all who among these labourers knew the family background of Pratima's mother or the circumstances under which she had lost her husband? Pratima had said, 'Mother does not allow me to work.' In retrospect, these two women inhabiting the same space followed entirely dissimilar modes of behaviour. Pratima's mother seemed to belong to a different league and Sukurmani, whose life journey, too, had certainly not been easy or smooth, clearly did not appreciate her. That chance encounter in Kurichu was the first and last time she saw Pratima.

Until recently seen riding around town on his mother's back or cuddled in her lap, Surju Tutu could now be observed measuring the length and breadth of Kanglung on his own two feet, holding the tip of his mother's finger. The grip of his small feet on the ground had no doubt strengthened. He could be identified from a distance holding some shiny piece of tin or paper, an empty cigarette packet or a matchbox tied with a woollen thread or string and dragging it behind him as he walked. In case these items were not available, he would pick up a deodar cone. Once she had asked Sukurmani to bring some cones; they were good for making a fire. This assignment kept Surju happily engaged for quite some time, and the porch of her house was soon heaped with a pile of cones.

'Memsaab, I am late today! Surju go back from half the way. Refuse to come with me!' Sukurmani's hassled and perspiring face belied her exasperation.

'Why?' she enquired, alarmed.

'I do not know why. He is angry for no reason. He says he will not come with me. Where and with whom do I leave him?' Sukurmani spoke more to herself than her.

The child had no doubt valid reasons to throw tantrums. It was true: if his mother's daily grind was demanding, Surju's was equally so if not more—the four-year old had to wake up and march out of bed early every morning, come summer, winter or rain. So as far as childish pranks and tantrums were concerned, it was quite understandable. But the growing speed of Surju's footsteps coupled with the artistry of his fidgety fingers was beginning to adversely affect his mother's everyday routine.

The boy's childish pranks and activities gradually began to have an unnerving effect on her neat and orderly life as well. One fine day she caught him peeing with rapt attention on a rose bush in her garden. Sometimes he would pluck a rose bud or flowers and scatter their petals or pieces of waste paper all over the corridor. The pristine whitewashed walls of her front veranda were bedecked with his elaborate pencil doodles and scrawls. Interestingly, all of these activities were usually performed to the accompaniment of a musical symphony of his own making. What marvelous fusion of music and destruction! Would the boy at all heed his mother once he grew up, she often wondered.

'Sukurmani, you shouldn't be taking such things lightly. Today you are laughing at his pranks, but you never know when things might go beyond your control and you have to repent for his actions.' Like many others, she shared the typical Indian trait of giving unsolicited advice on all occasions and in all circumstances, and hence she was always generous with her counsel when it came to Surju or Sukurmani. However, she also considered herself to be some kind of self-appointed guardian of this mother-son duo, something that was also voluntarily endorsed by Sukurmani.

'But what can I do, Memsaab? Sukurmani bemoaned. 'I am inside the house. I cannot see him when he does all such mischief. He does not listen to me!'

'How can he not listen to you?' she sternly retorted. 'I fail to understand how a four-year child does not listen to his mother.' Today she is swayed by the whims and pranks of her son; in yester years, by those of her son's father. No wonder any Tom, Dick and Harry could take liberties with her anytime, anywhere.

In prompt response to her homily, Sukurmani would shout a reprimanding 'Oye baba!' and Surju's musical symphony would come to a halt, at least for some time. This high-pitched, unrestrained melody was always a distraction as it invariably coincided with the time she would be preparing for her lectures.

After a long wait of more than a month, the first rose had at last blossomed on the creeper hanging from the pole of her porch. The air was redolent with its fragrance. The scent of these roses was said to attract snakes; quite a few people had in fact advised her to chop off the creeper. But oh, those delectable bunches of budding roses! She was willing to withstand the imminent threat of snakes just for the sake of those lovely, fragrant roses. Blooming with the first rays of the morning sun, however, that precious first rose of the season lasted precisely all of two hours. After Sukurmani's departure when she came out on the veranda overlooking her front garden, the sight of those velvety soft petals torn and scattered all over the veranda filled her with such intense gloom and melancholy that it lasted the whole day. She had experienced something similar the day she had climbed the four steep kilometres up the hill near Trashigang, only to be confronted by the closed doors of the lhakhang at the summit; the lama was nowhere in sight and they had to climb down the slope without paying obeisance to the deity. The rose could be the handiwork of no one else but Surju. She had had no other visitors that day.

She was about to sit down on the armchair in the veranda when her eyes caught sight of a broken door handle lying on the steps. Who could have brought it there? The next minute her eyes turned towards the front door—the handle was missing. Only then she realised that the screeching sound she had mistaken for Surju dragging about some fancied item in a bid to keep himself amused while his mother worked was in fact the sound of his masonry with the door handle. Less than one arm's length tall, what heights would this mite of a boy scale with his destructive mind once he grows taller! Hasn't it been said that a toddler's feet can be measured from its cradle? She waited impatiently for the next day to take this tiny rascal to task.

The next morning she delivered a full-length sermon to Sukurmani on the upbringing of a child. If she couldn't keep her four-year old under her thumb, how could she handle those burly Biharis and Bhutias? With such meekness and docility in her character, Sukurmani should never have ventured out of her own country in the first place. Advertently or inadvertently, she would be mentally comparing Sukurmani to herself. She, too, had ventured out to this land on her own and was put in a vulnerable position. Despite the obvious differences in the nature and quality of work, and the hierarchy, the challenges one confronts as a single woman are more or less identical.

'Sukurmani, make sure that Surju is with you inside the house while you are at work. Don't let him sit out in the veranda or anywhere else on his own. Sometimes he plucks the flowers. Now he has broken the door handle. There is no end to his mischief.'

'He not listen to me, Memsaab,' she responded in a resigned voice.

'Then *make* him listen to you. He has got to listen to you. If he doesn't, you have to be strict with him. If a four-year old does not listen to you today, do you think you will have any control over him in the years to come?'

The years to come...? But each and every day in Sukurmani's life was different from the other. Every morning arrived with new challenges.

She was yet to get over the untimely termination of the tiny budding rose when Surju Tutu swung into action on yet another mission.

The compound of her cottage offered an enchanting view, courtesy the Canadian Jesuits who were the first inhabitants of this cottage. The finely shaped Christmas trees standing in a row, the flowering shrubs, especially the rows of peacock-plumage coloured plants skirting the lawn, and right in the centre, the many different kinds of roses planted in oval-shaped beds, which had now turned into unkempt bushes for want of proper care—all these owed their existence to the former occupants. The site for the college where she taught, Bhutan's first college, was selected by these Canadian Jesuits after they had surveyed the entire region. It was a picturesque valley, a picture-perfect vista, and her cottage complemented the landscape. It was this eye-catching view that had first brought her to this quiet and secluded spot. Staying in this cottage was indeed a privilege.

That day after many days of persistent coaxing and cajoling, she had finally escorted the gardener to her compound. Every day she would implore him, 'Please Aadu, weed the rose plants in my garden.' But Aadu was not to be blamed for the neglect. In the entire college campus there was only one gardener. One wedding gown and ten brides in waiting, as they say, or one pomegranate and one hundred sick in queue. The poor gardener had his hands full maintaining the sprawling lawns and flowerbeds of all colours and hues scattered across the length and breadth of the campus. The whole town took pride in its beautiful college gardens.

Every society has its own code of values and ideals. The Buddhist Bhutanese also subscribe to their own lifestyle and philosophy, firmly foregrounded in religion. In this land of dzongs, zangdopelries, lhakhangs, gompas, monasteries, stupas, prayer flags, manis and mask dances, the mindset of a *peldon* or ideal Drukpa is intimately connected with Bhutan's history, religion and with its geographical landscape. They are a proud, independent, self-sustaining and self-reliant people with limited needs who would not depend on others for the fulfillment of these basic needs. It is not quantity but the emphasis on quality of life which they religiously adhere to. For the Drukpas, national gross happiness in lieu of national gross income is not some theoretical paradigm earmarked for seminars and conferences, but something which is put into practice in everyday life and living. These people who wear cloth woven by their own hands, live in self-built, colourful wooden houses, fill their bellies with self-grown crops and vegetables and cross the rivers, rivulets, hills and valleys on their two-legged wheels will certainly not depend on the services of a gardener for the upkeep of their personal gardens. In a place where there was no salon, no barber to cut hair, each Drukpa man and woman was skilled enough to give each other a hair cut; where there was no laundryman, every person did his or her own laundry; where there was no gardener, every house was surrounded with flowers—every ideal Drukpa served as his or her own gardener.

But the habits and lifestyle developed over many years cannot be dispensed with so easily, and so she had been on the lookout for the college gardener for months for the restoration of her garden. Perchance that day she saw him passing by right in front of her house and so she had whisked him in. He arranged for one or two cuttings of all the different varieties of roses in the rose beds and planted some of them on the borders of the lawn.

Master Surju Tutu had a wonderful time that day lending Aadu a helping hand. He stood ready on his toes to carry out the gardener's instructions. He would hand him the scissors, fetch water in the can, carry away the pruned twigs and branches of the plants and throw them, doing all the errands enthusiastically.

The gardener had instructed her to water the plants after two or three days when the cuttings had firmly taken root in the ground. Accordingly, she fixed the water pipe in the tap and was about to begin watering the plants when to her great dismay and surprise she saw there was no sign of any of them. All the carefully planted rose cuttings had disappeared! She found Surju and cajoled him to spill the beans. He pointed towards the cuttings he had uprooted and planted here and there in the lawn as per his good judgement. She was nonplussed. As the gardener had thrown away all the spare saplings, there was no hope of retrieving them. All his labour had literally gone to dust. 'Surju!' she shrieked at the top of her voice in anger.

Detecting the unusually harsh note in her voice, Sukurmani came out running from the kitchen.

'What he does, Memsaab?' she asked in some alarm.

'See for yourself what this slip of a boy has been up to! Where is he?' She looked around for the little rascal, who had promptly run off.

Positioned at a safe distance now, Surju was alternately looking at her, then at his mother and then at the self-planted cuttings with a bewildered expression on his face. At that moment she really felt like giving him a tight, hard slap on his cheek. The situation corroborated the predicament of the farmer who bemoaned that his bullock did not plough as much land as the quantity of grain it consumed. In lieu of the services rendered by the mother hen you feed the chicken and be prepared to bear with all its misdemeanours. Every day there was some new story.

This time, the pitch of Sukurmani's usual 'Oye baba!' was sharply raised. Surju stood and stared at his mother in disbelief without budging from his place. Perhaps this was the first time he had heard his mother raising her voice at him. There was some exchange of words between mother and son, following which the duo moved inside the house.

After finishing her work, Sukurmani picked up her bag and called out for Surju. When there was no response from him she went out to the front veranda, then to the backyard calling him. She went to the roadside, but there was no sign of him anywhere.

'Memsaab, I don't know where Surju goes.'

'Where can he go? He must be around.'

'No Memsaab, he is nowhere. I look everywhere. He not take breakfast also. I am never angry with him like this.' Sukurmani was almost in tears now.

Now she, too, was scared. This boy was Sukurmani's only hope, her lifeline. This woman runs from one end of town to the other, puts up with all the toil and trouble from dawn to dusk only for the sake of this boy. She was annoyed with herself. He is but a child. He cannot possibly remain idle sitting at one place with folded hands. Even if he had spoilt the plants in ignorance the heavens would not have fallen on her. Tomorrow when she leaves this place for good, will she be taking with her these flowers and trees that she is so passionate about? Were these rose plants more precious than human life? This behaviour of hers only reflected the typical hypocrisy she had herself always been so critical of. You go out of your way to pamper a rich man's puppy, but shun a poor child. It does not cost anything to speak a few affectionate words to a child.

Then why was it so very difficult for her to utter a few loving words to this fatherless child? The moment he saw her the poor boy would start fidgeting in nervousness and either give up the task he was engaged in or get up from his place like a thief caught red-handed. Please let him reach home safely today! She would be more careful and sensible in future. Her Drukpa neighbour was so much better than her. Just the other day he was holding Surju in his arms, unlike her, least bothered with his dirty clothes and running nose.

Now both Sukurmani and her Memsaab were out on the street in search of Surju. Where could he possibly go? Sukurmani's voice choked, 'He not eat anything today. Today he also not want to come with me. These days he always complains of headache in the morning.' Poor child, he must have caught the morning chill.

Exhausted and fraught with worry, when both of them came back to the cottage, they saw Surju standing quietly in a corner of the porch next to his mother's bag, waiting for her.

'Where do you go!' There was some heated exchange of 'Oye baba!... No baba!' and 'Amma!' following which they left the premises, with the mother firmly holding the child by the hand.

She watched the mother-son duo walk down to the end of the road until they vanished out of her sight. Theirs was a unique relationship which could not be confined within the normative. More than mother and son, they were each other's companions, playmates, support, shelter and so much more.

Another day when Surju could not find his mother, abandoning all his usual hesitation and reserve, he had come running and clung to her, frantically repeating, 'Amma! Amma!'

'What happened to your Amma? Where is she?'

That was the first time Surju had spoken directly to her, the fear and panic writ large on his face. 'Amma! ... Amma not there!' And like a flash of lightning the truth of Sukurmani's words had struck home: 'If something happen to me in this foreign land, where does he go? So I give him my father's name, Surju Tutu.'

Like in a game of police and thief, mother and son had been running around searching for each other in opposite directions. 'I look for him everywhere, Memsaab! Doonn't knowwee where he goes!' And then their mutual and total relief at the sight of each other. Once he was by his mother's side again, Surju was relaxed, reassured, his carefree confidence restored. As long as the boy was with his mother it did not matter to him where he was; homeland or foreign land, it made no difference.

It was perhaps Sukurmani's destiny to be perpetually implicated in some petty controversy or the other. The Indian housewife community of the town was annoyed with her because they saw her as the prime culprit for their crisis of domestic help. One day Sukurmani was taken to task by Mrs. Rajan for this very reason. Sukurmani had no one but her Memsaab to whom she could tell her side of the story.

'Memsaab, she tells me you work in all houses and you tell my maid not to work in my house. When do I say so, Memsaab? I do not talk to Norbo. Her brother finds work in Rungthung. This Norbo is no good. Also she is going home very late. One day I see her with a boy in the upper market.'

She got out of this imbroglio soon enough, only to be entangled in another, more complicated one. When Norbo quit her job, Sukurmani was held responsible. When Babu Moshai's maid demanded a hike, his irate accusing glance was turned on Sukurmani. But it was the Bhutanese maid of Mrs. Dorji who surpassed all in levelling allegations against Sukurmani.

One day her Drukpa neighbour crosschecked Sukurmani's credentials with her. 'Is your maid honest?' she asked her somewhat hesitantly.

'Yes, of course. She is just like family.' Perhaps she wished to hire Sukurmani and so was making the initial enquiries. But she was taken aback at her neigbour's response when she said, 'Yes, yes. This is precisely what I also told Choden.'

'You told Choden? But what did you tell her and why?' Choden was Mrs. Dorji's maiden name. She was a teacher in the primary school, and often visited her neighbour. She had talked to Mrs. Dorji once or twice. But why did her neighbour have to vouch for Sukurmani's honesty with Mrs. Dorji?

'There has been a theft at Choden's house,' her Drukpa neighbour informed. 'It is quite a substantial amount—three thousand rupees. First Choden suspected her maid since she is the one who babysits in her house. The maid did not accept the charge at first. Only when they threatened to hand her over to the police did she mention your maid's name—she said that she had deposited the money with your maid.'

There was no need to interrogate Sukurmani on this account. She saw a dishevelled Sukurmani rushing to her room with a dazed expression on her face.

'Memsaab, that Bhutia says he give me to the poolis. That girl who works in her house is saying she give me peesa. I ask her when she give me peesa? She is saying she give it to me to buy wool. I tell the Bhutia he can come to my room and see. That Bhutia say so many bad things to me!'

That whole day her mind was clouded by doubts and misgivings. As they say, there can be no smoke without fire. Could this maid of Mrs. Dorji have fabricated this whole tale of Sukurmani borrowing the money to buy wool? She remembered one day while she was knitting, Sukurmani had shown an interest, saying, 'I too make sweater for Surju.' Fortunately for Sukurmani, after much pressure and intimidation Mrs. Dorji's maid ultimately returned the money; otherwise Sukurmani's credentials as the prime accomplice of the culprit had already been established. Such a slip of a girl this maid, and even she knew that Sukurmani could be played as a soft target, that the goat could be butchered if the circumstances so required. Sukurmani was just a dumping ground; what difference did it make if you threw a handful of garbage on it or the whole lot? Someone accused her of stealing three thousand rupees; someone more greedy and cunning added a foetus to her uterus; the pile of garbage kept growing and rose into a mound so high that one day Sukurmani was buried alive under it.

Barring these few imbroglios and snags, however, the train of Sukurmani's life seemed by and large to be running on track. The money she earned from her work at two or three houses was sufficient for the twosome. Added to this were the perks she received from these families in the form of second-hand clothes and food leftovers.

Sukurmani had been at work for more than two hours, and yet she was in no hurry to leave.

'Sukurmani, don't you have to go today?' she asked from her room.

She mumbled something inaudible.

'Speak loudly. I can't hear you.'

'I ... I stay here for some time, Memsaab...?' Then, after a hesitant pause, 'That man comes here. He is checking.'

'From where does this man come?' If he was an officer from Project Dantak of the Border Roads Organisation, perhaps a word could be put in through some Indian officer.

'He comes from Trashigang. Bhutia man comes from Trashigang for checking.'

'Don't you have the work permit?' Sukurmani had told her she was working in GREF in her sister's name.

'We get it when we work in Greef,' she said.

'So what is to be done now? There must be some way out.'

'*Fain* has to be paid, Memsaab.'

'How much is the fine?' She could give her the amount if it wasn't much.

'He ask for too much. Where is so much money? The mason also says so.'

'Who is this mason?' So far there had been no reference to this mason in her talks.

'He work in Drukshiring.' Drukshiring was the name of the local Drukpa construction company.

'How much money in all has to be paid to this officer?'

'If I pay seven hundred rupees, it would do. Some officers not agree for seven hundred also. This is a new man. He never come here before.'

'You better approach all the families you are working for to help you.'

If Sukurmani were to stop working those Indian housewives would be the worst hit; but she wasn't sure if they would be willing to pay her the extra amount. This checking officer must be staying in town. Perhaps one of her Drukpa colleagues in college might know this officer, and a word could be put in to him. On second thoughts, however, she did not know Sukurmani's exact immigrant status in this country; even her name wasn't her own. She did not know for how long she had been living in this country as an illegal migrant. It was imperative for her to maintain some distance from these locals for her own sake. There must be hassles involved with this work permit.

'Now what are you going to do?'

'I go home late. He will leave in two-three days.'

So it was not such a serious problem after all. Once you face a problem, you also find a way out. Checking, bribing, hiding, paying fines, Sukurmani was quite familiar with all these activities, as was also reflected in her English vocabulary—permit, poolis, repot, dooty, fain—which was equally sound and impressive. If she intends to overstay just for a day in her house, fine.

The next day she forgot to ask Sukurmani about the checking officer. Sukurmani also did not broach the subject, and the matter was forgotten.

This incident occurred after a week. It was afternoon. She was waiting for Sukurmani to leave so that she could bolt the door and enjoy her afternoon siesta. But Sukurmani was apparently in no mood to leave. Usually she did not take so long to finish the chores.

'Sukurmani hurry up. It is one-thirty p.m.'

She mumbled something inaudible.

'What is that? I don't get you. Speak loudly.'

'Bhutia man asks me to leave the room.'

'Why?' She couldn't hide her annoyance. This woman was now getting on her nerves.

'Yesterday he make so much noise.'

'Who? You mean the Bhutia man, your landlord?'

'No, Memsaab. That Bihari come back leaving his wife home.'

'Oh, your neighbour? When did he come back?' She was under the impression that Sukurmani had overcome that nuisance for good.

'He come back last week. Yesterday he drink raasi too much. A man from Rungthung also come with him. Then he bang my door. Surju howls. Then Bhutia man come. He say ...' Her voice again dropped, becoming almost inaudible, 'He ask me to leave the room.' Wiping her hands nervously on her saree, Sukurmani stood hesitantly at the door of her room.

Before she could respond, she caught sight of a bag in the backyard. It must be Sukurmani's. She came out of her room to the gallery-cum-store room. It had been swept and mopped clean; the kerosene tin and other things had been neatly stacked in a corner. The outlines of Sukurmani's plan became all too clear: so she planned to move in here with Surju, to this gallery-cum-store; all she was waiting for was her Memsaab's customary nod. She was not amused. The situation reminded her of the Arab's camel who inches into his owner's tent bit by bit, eventually ousting the Arab out into the cold of the desert. If those ruffians disturbing Sukurmani at odd hours smelt her presence in this house, they might very well follow her here. How desperately and jealously she had guarded her privacy and solitude, even at the cost of earning the disaffection of her compatriots and tolerating their sarcasm and gossip for choosing to stay out of the expatriate colony. Surely not to be saddled with this woman along with her son and her paramours to boot! No. Before the problem acquired dimensions beyond her control, it was imperative to put an end to it.

She looked straight at Sukurmani and said, 'Pick up your bag and leave.'

Taken aback by the unfamiliar and unexpected terseness in her Memsaab's voice, Sukurmani was out of the room in no time with her bag and Surju.

Those few inspiring, encouraging words she had spoken to Sukurmani to boost her 'moral and spiritual strength' just a few days ago were like drops of rain on dry, parched land; the land was the same again—dry and parched. Like the jingle of bad coins in your pocket, of what use were those empty words for Sukurmani? Spoken with good intent and heard in good faith, their salutary effect, if any, lasted but a few days.

That day, the next day and for many more days to come, she was overcome with a seething sense of shame and guilt at her worldly wisdom and prudence. The woman must be virtually out on the streets with Surju. In Kanglung there was no bus stand, railway station, gurdwara, inn or even a rain shelter where the two of them could spend the night. What hell would have befallen her if the mother and child had stayed in her gallery for some time? There was a ravine nearby where they could have gone to answer the call of nature. Her main anxiety pertained to this daily task of easing oneself; there was only one washroom in her bungalow, that too adjoining the kitchen. And then there was the burden of feeding two extra mouths. But the cost of food was in a way immaterial; the real problem was the cooking gas. She had only one gas cylinder. She used the heater of course, but the power supply was irregular, there were too many power cuts. This act of charity could not exceed beyond a few words of sympathy and monetary help of a hundred or two hundred rupees at the most once in a while. This was not her native country after all. How was she to define her own identity? Noun: woman; adjective: single; status: working; category: middle class. Notwithstanding the elevation of her status to 'Memsaab' by Sukurmani, she entertained no illusions whatsoever about herself when she looked into a mirror. One small slip on her part, and her fellow Indian fraternity would make mincemeat out of her. Didn't she recognise the ever alert, censorious, prying eyes of her fellow country women? A full-time maid would give them sleepless nights. Why, just the other day, how Babu Moshai had flared up at her for something as petty as paying a little more than the rest of them to her maid? He had not minced words in cutting her down to size.

'You are single; you can afford it. But you will soon be out of this place. What about us, the less fortunate ones who have to stay back? Once the rate is hiked, we will be the affected party.' The unspoken bitterness and envy behind 'us, the less fortunate ones' was all too clear. Those on contracts at the college bore this grudge against the Colombo Plan professionals for their privileged status in terms of salary and other perks.

Seen more pragmatically, it becomes necessary for an average, single, middle-class woman to tread the middle path. Neither too high up, nor too low. If you ascend too high the risk of a fall is always implicit; and if you descend too low you are vulnerable to slip and fall flat on the floor. In many ways, Sukurmani was perhaps freer to lead life on her own terms as compared with her Memsaab for she was not governed by the same social mores and could blithely bypass them. Sukurmani may fancy her as some big shot by the size of her bungalow, but only the house owner knows the cracks in the walls. There was a spacious garden in front of her house sans gardener and four luxury cars parked outside; but these were nothing more than a pageant in terms of ownership.

She will now have to look for a new maid. What if she hired Norbo as a full-time help? On her visit to Kurichu, the girl had expressed her willingness to work for her in case Sukurmani left. But her hands and feet were full of freckles and moles; not only was the sight repulsive, it could be unhygienic. Pratima would be a better option. Yes, she could be employed. But she had said, 'Mother does not permit.' She would have to explore other options.

Winter was in full swing. One quilt was not enough against the biting cold. At midnight she got up from bed and took out a blanket from the cupboard. The chilly air kept sleep at bay. Her feet were ice cold. She often wondered, how do these feet measure temperature? Finally at two in the morning she got up, boiled some water for the hot water bottle and kept it in bed. Then she could get a little warm. In the absolute silence of a winter night in the hills, she heard a humming sound outside. It was the night watchman chanting '*Om mani padme hum*' on his vigil. She felt a sudden sharp lump in her throat. Here she was cold inside the room with a quilt and a blanket. In what godforsaken corner of the town must those two be on this cold night? If she had Sukurmani's old address, she could try to get the details from her Bhutia landlord, or perhaps from her fellow 'countryman' by whose courtesy the woman and her child had been thrown out on the street, hapless and homeless.

She was saved the hassle of searching for a new maid. A few mornings later, Sukurmani was back at work and she got busy cleaning the utensils stacked in the sink as usual. She tried to read Sukurmani's face carefully, but it was like a clean slate. Faces accustomed to new scripts being inscribed on them everyday become in due course of time discoloured like old black boards, and one cannot decipher what is written on them. Four months ago when she had started working for her, Sukurmani used to be quite robust and healthy. In just two days she seemed to have shrunk, and her mekhla hung loose on her waist.

Despite wanting to know Sukurmani's whereabouts during those two nights, she could not bring herself to ask. What would she gain? And what right did she have now to ask her? Once she had bolted the door on Sukurmani in her hour of crisis, where was the scope now for any kind of sisterly warmth in their relationship? Was there still someone who disturbed her at night? Could she arrive at some compromise with her Drukpa landlord? Neither did Sukurmani broach the subject, nor did she ask her anything. Did she get news of her father? Did he receive the letter she had written and posted to him? These and so many other questions would be on the tip of her tongue, but something always restrained her from opening her mouth. Sukurmani would come and straightaway get into the kitchen. Surju accompanied her sometimes, sometimes she came alone. Where and with whom did she leave Surju, she could not ask her. 'Pick up your bag and leave,' she had said. Sukurmani had given her a befitting answer. She did not utter a single word, fair or foul, her silence mocking her Memsaab's claims of superiority.

Captain Verma had thrown a party. Captain Verma had joined as the new Commanding Officer of Dantak only last month. To her delight he turned out to be from her hometown in India, and they even had some friends in common. In a foreign land you strike a cord even with a native bird. Whenever she spotted a raven here, she would fondly remember the jet black crows of her town. In a foreign land the grounds for introduction, acquaintance and friendship are generously extended; somewhere the bond of language, elsewhere those of state, country, religion, gender, single woman status, kinship. Here, belonging to the same hometown offered the closest grounds for bonding.

'Please feel free to seek my help anytime,' said Captain Verma. 'I would be delighted to be of any use. And anyway we shall be meeting quite often now that our unit is here for some time.' Suddenly it struck her: he is the CO of Dantak. He could help in accommodating Sukurmani in GREF. If not GREF, he could employ her in his house as a domestic so that she could be issued the work permit. This would be more than enough for Sukurmani. And it would lessen her own guilty conscience to some extent.

'Captain Verma, there is a maid who works for me; a widow with a small child. She is from Darranga. I don't exactly know her immigrant status. Earlier she worked in Rungthung. There was some internal problem there, so she had to quit the job and come here. I would be greatly obliged if you could register her in the GREF in Kanglung. She could work as a labour on your construction sites. And if that's not possible she could work as a domestic. Anything you could do to legalise her stay in Bhutan would be of enormous help.'

'I am sorry, but it will not be possible to adjust her here in Kanglung. Our unit is scheduled to move out from Kanglung next month. But she could be adjusted in Rungthung. Construction work there will take at least a year to be completed. You can ask her if she would like to move to Rungthung. It won't be a problem,' he assured her.

The next morning when she informed Sukurmani about the offer to move to Rungthung and obtain the much-needed work permit, she was not expecting the response she got.

'Cannot go to Rungthung. Can work in Greef here.'

Of late she had noticed a perceptible change in Sukurmani. Her usual listlessness and vulnerability bordering on helplessness was gone; she was now distinctly more self-confident and assertive. From her window she could see the mother and child approaching the house from a distance. Her gait was not as careless and clumsy as it used to be. Sukurmani walked briskly with quick, straight steps. Her hair was neatly done into an upturned bun. She was now more carefully dressed and her approach to her work was also more businesslike. Like the other maids she, too, would now be in a hurry to finish her work, wind up and leave.

'Why? Why can't you move down to Rungthung?' she asked her somewhat sternly, a sternness she owed to her recent acquaintance with Captain Verma and his position. 'Is it because of that rogue of a Bihari? Just let me know his name, and we shall see how he dare even look at you. We shall report the matter to your senior officer; I know him.' She remembered the maxim: does any woman throw away the skirt because of the lice in it? But Sukurmani may not be able to comprehend this mix of skirt and lice. Even so, how long could this foolish woman run around without a legal work permit, living in constant fear of the local as well as the Indian authorities? She was bound to get caught sooner or later.

When no answer was forthcoming, she said resignedly, 'All right. As you wish. But I say this because a senior GREF officer is known to me, and he could give you a job in GREF in Rungthung. I had asked him to find you work here in Kanglung, but that is not possible. Give it a second thought. You would be earning fifty or sixty rupees daily wages. And as you told me, you also get free ration and kerosene. How much do you earn here from these three houses where you work? The biggest advantage is that you would get a work permit. What if one fine day you are caught during a check?' How could this woman have such a short memory when just the other day she was running from that Bhutia officer checking for illegal migrants?

'I get work permit, Memsaab.' She was taken aback by Sukurmani's cool reply. So this was the crux of the matter.

'You have got the permit? When? Who got it for you? Didn't you say the permit would cost you seven or eight hundred rupees? Who gave you this money?' She darted so many questions at her in one go.

'The man who works in Drukshiring. That carpenter. He writes my name too with his men.'

'Who is he?'

'He is from there, my des.'

'Darranga?'

'No, Ranchi.'

Ranchi in Jharkhand, erstwhile Bihar. When did Bihar become her des? Why just Ranchi or Bihar, the whole nation was Sukurmani's des. Basically she was a Dumka from Jharkhand. This carpenter could also be a Dumka, and thus her country cousin. She was much relieved for Sukurmani now that her name was registered with the local construction company, which granted her a legal status; otherwise she was bound to get caught in the legal mess one day.

'Memsaab, we people are Dumka,' Sukurmani said suddenly.

'Yes, I know. You told me so once. So how come you moved to this part from that end of the country?'

'That is ... my father comes first to Darranga. There he works in field. Then we don't own land. So he carries water for those Bhutias.'

First it was the father who carried water. Now it was the daughter's turn to construct the road.

'There, I do not tie saree this way. Our marriages are with Dumkas only, Memsaab.' After a long interval there was again this old intimacy between them. How she had missed this camaraderie. Suddenly the thought struck her, if that carpenter too was a Dumka, could Sukurmani be married to him?

'Is the Drukshiring carpenter also a Dumka?'

'No, he is from Ranchi. My des.'

'You mean from Darranga?'

'No, no. From Bihar.'

But how could Bihar be her des? Had she already forgotten that 'ssala' Bihari? And then she recalled—Sukurmani's family had moved to Darranga from Kokrajhar after the tribal feuds there. It was true; the borders of her des and the corresponding national boundaries encompassed a larger India where a Bodo from Assam or the north-east or a Dumka from Jharkhand could fondly identify a Bihari as her countryman with such strong feelings of kinship. This fellow countryman of hers must indeed be a gentleman to help her with the permit.

'These days Surju does not come with you. Where do you leave him?' She had for long wanted to ask her this. Despite his frequent mischiefs and pranks, she missed the boy. He brought some life and energy to her quiet house.

'He stay with the carpenter at home. He do his work, Surju sit nearby. He watch him, help him.' The thought of the child sitting by the side of the carpenter brought a smile on the mother's face. As she fondly recounts her child's pranks, every mother is a Yashoda and every mother's darling is the eternal mischievous Krishna Kanhaiya, on whose pranks all of Gokul doted. For her precious Surju, Sukurmani was not only mother, aunt and sister, she was also father, brother, uncle, friend and playmate. Yashoda, Devaki, Nand, the Gopis, the cowherds who played with Krishna—Sukurmani was all of these. If anyone doted on Surju, it was she; if anyone fed him, it was she; if anyone worried if he was out of sight too long, it was she; if anyone chided him, which was rare, it was again she.

'He make a cart for Surju. Yesterday the whole day Surju drag the cart. Not sleep at night. Say he sit in the cart,' Sukurmani recounted, her eyes shining with laughter and love for her son.

'Does this carpenter stay near your house?' she asked hesitantly.

'He stay with us in our *quartar*,' was the frank answer.

'Do you stay with him?' So finally this was the secret of Sukurmani's clean saree, her neatly tied bun and this fellow countryman's 'gentlemanly' behaviour.

'We do not stay with him in his room, Memsaab,' Sukurmani clarified with a slight edge to her voice. 'He give us room to stay.'

'Good, you better stay out of him. Be careful, otherwise you will again be inviting trouble for yourself.' Homeless and kinless in a foreign land, if anything untoward was to happen to this foolish woman, where would she find refuge with one more belly to fill?

As if she had read both her mind and her veiled warning, Sukurmani said, with a hand over her abdomen, 'I have problem here, Memsaab.'

'How do you know?'

'When Surju is born, then she tell me. She knows.'

'Who is this she?'

'She who make delivery.'

Sukurmani's English vocabulary was simply marvelous! Delivery, fain, permit, market, distub, late, India, brekfast, dooty, repot, quartar, registar and God knows what else. English, the global language of mobility and empowerment—if only it could also empower Sukurmani! Anyhow, if there was some problem with her uterus, as she said, under these circumstances it was probably a blessing in disguise. Whatever be the means, she had at long last been able to procure the work permit on her own. How could she say that Sukurmani was not self-sufficient and self-reliant?

These days, Sukurmani exuded a pleasant aura of brisk cheerfulness. Instead of the usual heavy clumsiness of her gait, as if she were dragging a dead weight, there was a litheness and agility, a distinct sprightliness in her step. Sometimes she even had a vague feeling as if Sukurmani's eyes followed her silently with a tinge of pity in them.

That day she had a severe headache and had been laid up in bed since morning with her head tied up.

'You have headache, Memsaab?' Bending over her pillow, Sukurmani touched her head tenderly and enquired, 'Take medicine?'

'No.' Her stock of pills was exhausted and with this headache she could not walk down to the dispensary.

'Yes, being alone how you can bring medicine? I will inform that other memsaab, your friend. She bring you medicine. Memsaab, you will be here in Kanglung for some more time?'

'No. We are due for our summer vacations after two months. Six months after the summer vacations, I shall have the final break. Then I shall go back to India.' Suddenly it struck her that Sukurmani had asked her a personal question after a long time. It was not in Sukurmani's nature to be inquisitive. She never asked for any favours. Even when the gap between life and death was narrowed to a few days or hours, this woman maintained a heroic silence.

Next month was Durga Puja. She must gift Sukurmani a nice sari. Last year the whole year all her enquiries were centred around Durga Puja. Durga Puja at her home in India, Durga Puja in Rungthung, and now Durga Puja in Kanglung.

It was dusk when the door bell rang. Before she could get up and open the door, it rang again. Who could be so impatient? When she opened the door, a distraught Sukurmani stood there.

'Memsaab, Surju comes here?' she asked, her anxious eyes searching the room.

'No, he hasn't come here. But he was not with you this morning either.'

'I don't know where he goes.' Sukurmani looked pale with worry. 'He is at home in the afternoon. He is busy doing work. He think Surju must be there in our room. Then he does not see him. Where he goes?'

This 'he' was obviously the Drukshiring carpenter. 'Where could Surju go? He must be around,' she said to console her. 'Go and ask at Sanju's house. Perhaps he is playing there with Sanju,' she suggested although she knew quite well that there was little chance of Surju playing with Sanju so late in the evening. Sukurmani left, running down the stairs. A man stood waiting at the gate and joined her as she walked down the road. He must be the Drukshiring carpenter. His refined bearing and persona belied his class; he was certainly in a different league from Sukurmani. But class hierarchy apart, what mattered most right now was this man's presence by her side in her hour of crisis. Otherwise right now she would be searching the lanes and bylanes of Kanglung alone for her child. Then a contradictory thought crossed her mind: wasn't this man directly or indirectly responsible for the boy going missing? Hadn't the child run outdoors due to his negligence? He must have been too busy at work to notice when the child slipped out.

That whole night she tossed restlessly as thoughts of Sukurmani and Surju preoccupied her sleepless mind. Where could the boy possibly have gone? Perhaps someone had taken him along with them; he was so vulnerable. Children like him were so often the victims of child trafficking and abuse of all kinds. Herself an illegal migrant, where and with whom was Sukurmani to register her complaint if the child went missing. This boy was one troublemaker. Couldn't sit idle for a minute in one place. Always into some mischief or the other. And his adoring mother would never scold him. But there was no denying that the child was a carefree bird. Such expressive eyes. He may not utter a word but those eyes said everything—his complaints, affection, explanations, apologies—everything. What emotion was there that those eyes could not communicate without words? And he was content to be by himself; he did not need a playmate. His mother may be busy with her chores, Surju could happily pass his time feeding the birds, chasing butterflies, inspecting the fallen branch of a tree, a sapling or a vehicle, collecting pine cones, or just singing to himself.

Next morning sharp at seven, mother and child were present on duty as if nothing had happened the previous day. All of a sudden she felt a surge of affection for this boy. In this alien land, her day began with the sight of this duo. Apart from Sukurmani and Surju, who was really there for her to talk to?

'Where did you disappear yesterday, Surju?' she asked, caressing him fondly. Those big eyes stared at her unblinking, as if demanding an explanation from her instead and saying: Why can't you always be nice to me like this? The mother was delighted at this unexpected display of affection and concern from her Memsaab.

'He goes to lower market to get ghaslet. Then that Rungthung Bathar comes home. Surju knows Rungthung Bathar, so he goes with him to upper market. I do not see him so I worry. I say where he goes?'

So the Drukshiring carpenter was not to be blamed after all. Somehow deep inside her, she wanted to be able to trust this Drukshiring man, more for Sukurmani's sake than anyone else's.

'Yesterday, the man who stood at the gate, he accompanied you. Is he the carpenter of Drukshiring?'

'Yes, Memsaab. He come with me.'

'Did he help you get the work permit?'

'Yes. He write my name there in *registar*.'

'What is his name?'

'Basant.'

So their acquaintance had progressed up to the exchange of first names. Well, his name and his looks were both impressive. Still, there were a few gaps she could not quite fill in. What did this man see in Sukurmani, a single mother of a son? She was probably older than him too.

'He too is single; no wife and children. Does not make marriage. Come here long time back from his country.' Sukurmani, as if reading her mind, provided an update on her beau. Then after a pause, she suddenly blurted out, 'He ask me to make marriage.'

Foolish woman! If she hadn't seen the Drukshiring carpenter, she could have perhaps believed Sukurmani. A woman's physical appearance, her attractiveness, complexion, age—for a man these were usually the defining variables for a marriage. And then this woman was also saddled with a child. If only she could give Sukurmani a mirror to look at herself closely at least once in the morning. Not alone, but with Surju. Did she really understand the meaning of 'making marriage'? For the man it did not mean taking responsibility for Sukurmani alone; after all she was the milking cow and could earn enough to fill her belly, but this cow had to be accepted with her calf. However, Sukurmani seemed completely confident of herself in this matter. Her only regret in the end was that she erred in her choice of partner.

'He must be fooling you, Sukurmani. You better watch out,' she responded tersely and went into the washroom. There was no point arguing with her. No one could put any sense into her foolish head. Make marriage indeed!

After finishing her work, Sukurmani sat down on the stairs of the porch.

'Yesterday, Runthung Bathar comes, Memsaab.'

Surju's going off with this Bathar to the market yesterday was what had caused all the confusion and panic. Sukurmani referred to this man quite often. Rungthung Bathar, Kanglung Bathar. Bathar said this, Bathar said that. Bathar had assured her of help in getting Surju admitted to school. Bathar would also enquire about Sukurmani's wellbeing occasionally. But just who this Bathar was she still had not figured out.

'Who is this Bathar you keep talking about? Did he also work in Rungthung with you all?'

'No, Memsaab. Bathar does not work with us. He lives in Darranga,' Sukurmani replied, half smiling at her ignorance. 'He does not work with us. Some of his men work with us. Bathar come to ask for them.'

Perhaps he was some kind of contractor who supplied labour to the GREF. This could also be the reason for his frequent visits to the nearby towns where the construction labourers lived in camps. Whoever this Bathar was, he was clearly a man of some substance.

'Memsaab, Surju's baba also tell me not to do too much work.' By now she too had accepted the existence of this Drukshiring carpenter in Sukurmani's life. As to how and when he was promoted and given the honorific of 'Surju's baba' she did not quite remember. Every time she used this honorific 'Surju's baba' to refer to Basant, the supreme contentment writ large on Sukurmani's face reminded her of the mother's expression when she called her child for breakfast with an 'Oye baba'. Not just breakfast, the resourceful mother had now successfully procured a handsome, reliable, five feet ten inches tall young 'father' for her son.

Meanwhile, Sukurmani had also found work at her colleague Mrs. Mitra's house. Like her, Mrs. Mitra also stayed alone; her children were in college and so could not accompany her to Bhutan. She had soon formed an intimacy with her. Intellectually enlightened, broadminded and sensitised, unlike most others here, Mrs. Mitra's attitude towards prevailing social and moral norms was not conventional. The same broadminded generosity was also reflected in her attitude towards Sukurmani, who became the go-in-between her and Mrs. Mitra in their exchange of occasional treats and delicacies.

While their conversation invariably centred around Sukurmani, references to Basant were inevitable. Mrs. Mitra, who hailed from Ranchi, had worked closely with the tribal women of Jharkhand as part of her research project. She was both well informed and well acquainted with the ways and customs of the tribal women of those parts, especially Dumka women.

'Stop fretting so much about Sukurmani,' Mrs. Mitra said to her one day. There is no need for you to worry about her. Dumka women do not have such inhibitions about their sexuality; they exult in it. Their point of view on sex differs from that of yours or mine.'

There must be some truth in her statement. So many times she had been aware of Sukurmani silently watching her from the corner of her eyes. She could read the thoughts behind those curious, pitying eyes: A single woman; what a monotonous life this Memsaab leads. No one to get her medicine for a headache or sickness. Pining all alone in such a huge bungalow. No friends, no company. True; from Sukurmani's point of view she was verily a pitiable, deprived soul for being denied physical pleasures and the company of men.

She often wondered, how old must Sukurmani be? Twenty-seven or twenty-eight at the most? One day when she had asked her, the reply was, 'All that we people not know, Memsaab.' Sukurmani had suffered two major bereavements—her husband and daughter—very early in life. She had moved to Kanglung after living with a Bihari in Rungthung for about a year or so. And now she was in a similar relationship with this carpenter of Drukshiring. If this Basant also turned out to be like that Bihari of Rungthung, what Sukurmani's predicament would be was anyone's guess. Sukurmani's response towards the reticent and reserved mother of Pratima had been one of pity and disapproval: 'She does not talk to anybody in a smiling way. Does not go anywhere.' But as Mrs. Mitra rightly said, we cannot judge tribal folk by our middle-class norms and standards; they have their own. When Sukurmani had tried to lead her life in conformity with middle-class social norms, she was virtually thrown out on the streets to perish with her child. Without the work permit, by now she would have been dragged beyond the Bhutan gate in Samdrup Jonkhar into Rangia within Indian territory. At this critical juncture of her life, this Drukshiring carpenter was her only hope and saving grace. And where would he too find a nubile virgin in this remote, secluded place? Far from their land, home, family and kinsfolk, exhausted after the day's toil, these labourers too are entitled to a few hours of leisure and pleasure. Some find comfort in a bottle of home-brewed Bhutanese arra or Indian raasi, others with the likes of Sukurmani. Given such tough and rough living conditions, their ways of life are bound to differ.

This glimpse into the life of these migrant labourers, and her newfound worldview, she owed to her maiden visit to Kurichu. The parameters of our judgement are determined by our social milieu and social conditioning, which contribute a specific mindset and value system. Unexposed to different and disparate lives and human behaviour, one tends to be judgmental. The sight of those labourers working at that desolate construction site in Kurichu against the backdrop of that vast dreadful silence of nature had triggered a momentous realisation—in that moment she was no longer just a passive, objective spectator but could empathise with those labourers from a subjective viewpoint. In that epiphanic moment, she saw the superfluity of those cherished beliefs, ideas and preconceived notions that she had so long adhered to and taken pride in. In this alien and intimidating environment far from human habitation when you confront nature in its most raw and primitive form, the modes and modalities of human social intercourse and behaviour take a somersault.

As for the present, Sukurmani was happy and content. Basant, the carpenter of Drukshiring, must also be presumably. And what about Surju? Whether or not he shared his mother's happiness she could not say, but she did notice his frequent mood swings these days. The boy had turned out to be quite willful and stubborn.

The imported cars parked in her compound were of great attraction for the children. Drukpa or expatriate Indian, all of them would automatically stop by and admire them. If no one was in sight, they would feel bold enough to touch these cars, inspect them from all sides with wistful, longing eyes. Quite often the young mothers taking their children for a walk would show them these vehicles and point out by way of adding to their general knowledge: 'My dear this is a Hylax. That one is Toyota Corona. No, no baby, this is not a car, this is a jeep.' Usually this is how she was also introduced to the children, 'Baba, do you know this aunty? She is the one who stays in that big house where those beautiful cars are parked. Say hello to her.' And instantly she would meet their eager, appreciative glances, their palms folded in a respectful *Namaste*. If the child was smart and bold enough, he or she would even add, 'Aunty I would like to ride that car.'

'Sanju is always willing to come to your place,' or 'Please do come and visit us some time. We are always the ones visiting you. Even if we stop him, Vikki always brings me to your compound!'

That day when she looked out of the window, she saw Surju carrying a tin full of water. Perhaps he was going to water the plants. But oh no! The very next minute he went and threw the muddy water with full force on the windscreen of the SUV! She ran out of the house towards the car before he could hit the mudguard with the empty tin. Good heavens! This boy was so unpredictable and destructive sometimes! Donated by the World Wildlife Organization, this was the most expensive vehicle in the campus. The other older cars and jeeps had been parked elsewhere. These relatively new and expensive vehicles were parked outside her bungalow from a security point of view. She snatched the tin from Surju's hand and dragged him inside the house. Until now his mischief had been limited to plucking flowers, uprooting plants or drawing on the walls. Had there been even a small dent or scratch on that car worth fifteen or twenty lakhs, she would have had to answer for it. This slip of a boy could be such a nuisance!

'Sukurmani, I have told you so many times, make Surju sit here with you. Make sure he doesn't budge an inch out of your sight. Does he take those cars for his playthings!'

For the first time Surju's mother shared her sentiments. 'He does not listen to anyone, Memsaab. I do not know what he does. At home also he is same. Surju's baba also angry with him. Yesterday when he works, Surju bolts him from outside. He cannot come out from his room and is very angry.'

Those large expressive eyes of Surju staring intently at his mother—how to read them? There was anger, hurt, insult and humiliation in those eyes, but no contrition. Though she had always warned Sukurmani to be strict with Surju, today the harshness in the mother's tone towards the child brought a lump to her throat. Behind that harshness and censure, she could also hear the backing of 'Surju's baba.' Otherwise till date all caution and advice to Sukurmani regarding Surju had fallen on deaf ears. The Drukshiring carpenter had undoubtedly ended Surju's monopoly over his mother. At times she could hear a note of complaint and angry hurt in Surju's high-pitched calls of 'Amma!' From Sukurmani's neatly tied saree and upturned bun, her eyes would turn to Surju's dirty, shabby clothes. If you love me, you must also love my dog—wasn't the Drukshiring man familiar with this maxim? You throw crumbs to the dog for a few days, and once you have earned its affection and loyalty, you are done with it? True; in a man-woman relationship there was no need for secrecy or clandestine behaviour. But then Sukurmani's relationships with men had never exactly been a secret in Rungthung or in Kanglung for that matter. Mrs. Mitra was right; the mindset of these folks was different.

Nevertheless, for the time being at least, the Drukshiring carpenter's presence had brought some colour to Sukurmani's drab life. And the change was visible not just in her self-assured, relaxed and carefree mien. A big round *bindi* adorned Sukurmani's forehead these days. Her face had rounded up. She had also gained weight and now worked in only two houses—Mrs. Mitra's and hers. A more observant and seasoned feminine eye would have gauged the secret of her weight-gain soon enough, but she did not. Consequently she had to be embarrassed at her neighbour's remarks.

'When is she expecting?' her Drukpa neighbour asked her casually one day during conversation.

'Expecting? Who is expecting?' She was taken aback by the query.

'Your maid Sukurmani, of course. Didn't you know?'

'Well ... no. Actually I didn't notice,' she fumbled.

'What does her husband do? I think he works in Drukshiring. The other day I saw him at the construction site of that new building.'

'Do you know him?'

'No. But I have seen this man there. Your maid's son—what's his name...? Yes, Surju—I have also seen the boy in that building with this man.'

Construction work was in progress in that new building. When Surju did not accompany Sukurmani to work, he would be with the Drukshiring carpenter. One close look at Sukurmani, and it was obvious she was pregnant. She felt so stupid.

'Didn't you say you had some problem with your uterus? Now what are you going to do with this child?' she asked Sukurmani the first thing next morning without any preliminaries.

'Surju's baba say no abortion. I say I go to Trashigang and abort it. He is very angry. He tell me not to do much work these days.'

So this was the actual reason for Sukurmani's refusal to go to Rungthung. All these things were beyond her knowledge and understanding. There used to be maidservants in India as well, but Sukurmani belonged to such a different world. Nirmala, Kamala, Bala, the lot of them had their own share of problems: putting up with drunkard husbands; taking care of the children; sharing the financial burden of their families; managing the homes of their memsahibs as well as their own to the best of their ability; some even enjoyed the washing machines, refrigerators and geysers of their employers, and occasionally added spice to their own lives as well as that of their memsahibs as gossipmongers and informers. But Sukurmani's life was so unlike theirs.

'Who else is there in this carpenter's family?' she asked Sukurmani.

'He too is alone. Leaves home many years back. Comes here to work. So he does not make marriage.'

There seemed to be no common grounds of compatibility, appearance or status between the two, except for the fact that 'He too is alone.' But if he had stopped her from aborting the child, as Sukurmani claimed, and restrained her from working in more than two houses, perhaps he was indeed serious about her and the baby in her womb. He was either a gentleman or some unfortunate wretch like Sukurmani. Who knows what qualities of Sukurmani had endeared her to him? A poor, lone, gullible, vulnerable woman struggling to make ends meet in an alien land with her child. But perhaps he had been moved by pity for her for this very reason. Whatever it was, all her beliefs, values and preconceived notions on this matter were in jeopardy here. As far as Sukurmani and her ilk were concerned, Mrs. Mitra was right: in a life so dictated by circumstances beyond your control and so full of uncertainty, flexibility was essential for survival.

Ten days on was Durga Puja.

'Sukurmani, Durga Puja is almost here.'

'Yes. After ten days is Durga Puja,' Sukurmani said flatly in a voice devoid of expression. Perhaps she was tired. This time she must gift her a saree. Then another thought crossed her mind: now that the Drukshiring carpenter was there to present her with a new saree, she should better buy some clothes for Surju instead to replace those shabby, dirty ones that he perpetually wore.

'Sukurmani, come along with me to the upper market in the evening. Let's buy some new clothes for Surju.'

'He also say so.'

These days Sukurmani must be able to save up some money. 'Who meets the expenses at home?' she asked her casually.

'He also spend, I also spend. He bring ration from market.'

'What other expenses are there if he buys the ration?' This simpleton must not be fooled.

'Rent is there, Memsaab.'

How much would the room rent be, she wondered, but didn't ask.

'Does he drink?'

'No,' Sukurmani said emphatically. 'He does not drink. Take very nicely meat and fish.' After a pause she added, 'Many people come to him. They all eat with us too.'

All this information was disconcerting. She had a gut feeling that there was something rather fishy in this whole affair. With a natural apathy and lack of sympathy towards men in general, she instinctively suspected the intentions of the Drukshiring carpenter and those of his coterie. This time she would not hand over Sukurmani's wages to her, she decided, but keep them aside for her.

She also made a mental resolution not to make any further enquiries about the Drukshiring man henceforth, nor to listen to anything related to him. This was Sukurmani's life; she will have to bear the consequences of her actions and decisions. There was an old saying: never ask directions for a village road you are not going to take. In another six months her term here would be over. Then she and Sukurmani would part ways, and it was unlikely that their paths would ever cross again. This was a small town in another country with just a handful of fellow country people, so one got interested in each other's affairs. This was for the first time in her life that she had become so involved in the personal life of another individual, that too a maid.

And so she had stopped making personal enquiries of Sukurmani for some time. Otherwise she would have learnt the truth earlier. For the past few days, Sukurmani seemed rather lackluster and out of spirits. Gone was the lately acquired sprightliness and neatness of bearing and she was once again draped in her old saree. On top of it she had wrapped around an unmatched, moth-eaten shawl, presumably to hide her advanced state of pregnancy. She could have given a spare shawl to Sukurmani, but unlike in the past she no longer felt responsible for the woman. Only if she were married could she empathise with a pregnant woman. It is rightly said, how can a barren woman feel labour pains?

'Sukurmani, is everything all right? Do you eat properly?' she asked her half indifferently one day, and at once so many other questions cropped up in her mind: what about pre-delivery checkups, proper diet, adequate rest, precautions, and most importantly, who would deliver her child? There was no hospital in Kanglung, although local midwives must be available. And then Sukurmani interrupted her train of thoughts.

'Memsaab, it is more than two weeks when Surju's baba goes to his des. He does not come.'

So he had fired the last shot. She was hardly surprised. In fact she had all along anticipated this. Sukurmani stood there in the same crushed, faded old saree. It could just be her imagination, but after a long time the mother-son duo seemed to be once again complementing each other as in the old days. The neat upturned bun, the soft radiance of her face had all vanished; only the bindi was intact in its place on her forehead.

The manager of the Drukshiring construction company was a Keralite. When she enquired about the carpenter Basant, he expressed ignorance and said no man with this name was employed in his company. Only when she explained to him the delicacy of the situation, he replied, 'Okay, so that woman works for you? Yes, she also has a son. That man, yes he was staying somewhere in the upper market. But his name is not Basant; he was called Latif. He has left my company and gone to Thimphu.'

'Do you have his address with you?'

'Madam, you never know what fake name he must have taken there now. I could give you the names of one or two construction companies in Thimphu, and perhaps you could find out his whereabouts from them, although the chances are few.'

So Sukurmani knew that he was a Muslim.

'Why did you tell me that his name was Basant?' she asked Sukurmani the next day.

'Ssala! He only tell me so in the beginning, Memsaab!'

Well then now face the music. But Sukurmani was still hopeful of his return. 'He does not take any luggage, Memsaab.' If not for her, at least he might come back for his things.

There was another maid who worked for Mrs. Mitra now. This was Pratima; her mother was sick, so she could not afford to sit at home. She said that the Drukshiring carpenter, Latif alias Basant, was working in Kurichu sometime back and that he had brought his family for a short visit to Kurichu once, and that Sukurmani knew about it. Was Sukurmani then lying to her all along about his credentials, or did she really not know? 'He alone, I alone,' could it all have been fake? But despite evidence to the contrary, she still wanted to believe Sukurmani.

First Durga Puja in Kurichu; the second one in Rungthung with the Bihari; the third in Kanglung with Latif. And the fourth one...?

Why only blame Latif, she, too, was Sukurmani's culprit. This crisis in Sukurmani's life could probably have been averted; if not averted at least it could have been postponed for a time had she offered them shelter in her store room on that crucial day. For then Sukurmani may not have sought the carpenter's help and paid such a heavy price for it. Now what was in store for this woman and her two children, one in the womb, God alone knew.

Sukurmani left no stone unturned to trace the Drukshiring carpenter, making an endless number of phone calls to Thimphu from two or three numbers through the Bathar, but to no avail.

'Memsaab, he comes if boy is born,' she said more to reassure herself than her Memsaab.

Who says that the parameters of life and social standards for people like Sukurmani are any different from those of the middle class? The wheel of Sukurmani's hope now revolved around three focal points: 'Thimphu', 'boy' and 'luggage'. Latif could be traced if someone could go to Thimphu; the news of the birth of a boy would surely bring him back to her; and he might come back to collect his luggage. That feeling of utter desperation and impatience—if only she could go to Thimphu. For now all roads lead to Thimphu. Which bus leaves for Thimphu from Trashigang at what time, which truck leaves for Thimphu when, Sukurmani had up-to-date information on all these details. However, as an experienced migrant she also knew that residing in Kanglung without a work permit for a few days was one thing, but travelling to the capital Thimphu without official work or without a legal work permit was not child's play.

She did not have to tell Sukurmani about her forthcoming visit to Thimphu.

'Memsaab, you people go to Thimphu.'

'Yes. I was going to tell you.'

'For how many days you go?'

'It is a two-week programme. I will be out for a fortnight.'

'Memsaab, if you ask there in Thimphu, you can find him...?'

Yes, but whom could she ask about this absconding man? She only had a fleeting glimpse of this Latif alias Basant; when Surju had gone missing he had escorted Sukurmani in search of him. That desperation on Sukurmani's face when she was loading her suitcase and bag on the bus to Thimphu—were she not a human being but some article, she would have packed herself along with the luggage! Sukurmani was due for delivery anytime; otherwise she had seriously considered discussing with the authorities the possibility of taking Sukurmani along with her to Thimphu. If only it were in her power to do so. 'Ssala!' From the elevated position of 'Surju's baba,' Latif had been unceremoniously downgraded to 'ssala.' Interestingly, right till the end, Sukurmani had no regrets for 'making marriage.' Nor did she seem unduly worried about the fate of the child in her womb or the hassles she would face in bringing it up. Her only regret was that she had not made the right choice in marriage. Otherwise, there was a long queue of admirers waiting for her hand!

'Memsaab, so many men come from Rungthung to take me. A man comes from Kurichu also. I think this man is good because he does not drink raasi.' Sukurmani herself had brewed this raasi so many times and offered it to so many men. 'He does his work in good way. He talk to we people also in good way. With Surju also he talk in good way, sometime give him *chaklate* also. So I think Surju have someone in this foreign land.'

That typical patriarchal mindset. A woman's dependence on man for one reason or another. Sukurmani's anxiety for male presence and protection in her life exhibited the same mindset that inculcates in a woman an inborn instinct to be dominated by men. First her father's name was to be the protective umbrella for her son; then this newfound 'Surju's baba' was added to her life so that her son had a father figure in this foreign land.

'Sukurmani, you better go back to your own country, or it will be too late. If you fear *himsa* from your brother, you go to the village of Surju's baba. There you can be with your own people.'

'There my sister's man still does not make marriage. If I go, he be very happy.'

'Why don't you go then? I shall make arrangements for your travel.' So long as Captain Verma was in Dantak, deporting Sukurmani to Darranga in any of the army trucks was not a big deal.

'I cannot go there, Memsaab. My sister's husband takes too much raasi. Then he does too much *himsa*. That is why my sister dies.'

Right till the very end, the multidimensional facets of this *himsa* remained elusive and incomprehensible to her.

'Sukurmani, listen to me carefully. Be it the Rungthung Bihari or the Drukshiring carpenter, no man will ever marry you, do you understand? Never!' But this harsh homily was lost on her like the chant of some indecipherable mantra.

If only this woman understood how temporary diasporic relationships are formed and knew that they are always determined by external circumstances. Why just Sukurmani, all the Indian and other expatriates posted on short-term assignments and contracts were caught in the same web of temporariness; once their term was over they would all be heading back. Some labourers could keep their families with them for short intervals; others like the Drukshiring carpenter lived alone, and women like Sukurmani fitted well into their short-term planning; she was an easy option for securing temporary warmth and pleasure. Who would marry a woman with a child, now, of course two? If you intend to stay here, you have to be like Pratima's mother—only because she did not talk to anyone or smile at them, she and her daughter were still safe. Sukurmani, how will you work in GREF now with an infant to care for? By putting your child to sleep by the roadside? The Bihari and Nepalese women labourers in India also manage to survive this way.

Sukurmani's confidence, her self-assurance, agility, poise and the softness of her face all had vanished along with the Drukshiring carpenter Basant alias Latif. She was back to being her usual uncertain, hesitant self.

'Memsaab, Bathar says he take us there with him. There is school also. During the day children get *brekfast* and also milk. If you sick, there is also hospital. If there is work, I can work. But how I can go now? After this delivery I go there with Bathar.'

The generosity of this Bathar without any apparent personal interest or motive was intriguing. At the same time, she was annoyed with Sukurmani. If such an advantageous option was available to her, why didn't this foolish woman go back to Darranga with the Bathar in the first place? No wonder this woman had got used to loafing around.

'Is that Bathar single?' She tried to unearth the cause of his generosity.

'No, he has with him his children. His wife know delivery work.'

There she stood with Surju by her side and her big protruding belly. As long as Sukurmani remained in this town in this alien country, she would always be easy prey to some Bihari or Latif or the other. She could surely find employment as a labourer on some road in her own country as well. Your own country after all is your own.

'Sukurmani, shall I talk to the officer in GREF on your behalf? Everyday the army trucks ply to Darranga. You could go up to Darranga in one of these vehicles.'

'They ask for permit.' The same old excuse.

'Didn't I tell you not to worry about the permit? It will be arranged.'

Her eyes fixed on the ground, Sukurmani was engrossed in thought for a while. Then she said, 'How I go there? No money. I am here for two Durga Puja. There my dada do too much *himsa*. Do not know how my father is.'

'Then you go to the village of Surju's baba.'

'There women in Surju's baba's house do not give us food. They all do *himsa* to Surju.' She again lapsed into silence. Then she said, 'He come here, Memsaab. I know he come if a boy is born. His luggage is also here.'

As long as there is breath, there is hope. Sukurmani had not given up hope that the Drukshiring carpenter would come back to her if a boy was born to her. If not for the boy, he might return to claim his luggage. Perhaps Sukurmani's father Sarju Tutu was also keeping alive some such impossible hope of the return of his daughter who had gone to a foreign land to make money.

'The Bathar also tell us to wait. I do not give room rent. The Bhutia allows us to stay for sometime.'

'Not paid the room rent? But didn't you say that he was the one who paid the rent?'

'No, he not pay rent for two month. Take all money home.'

'And you gave him *all* the money?'

'He bring ration.'

But how much would the ration cost, didn't she even know this much? 'Didn't he give you any money at all?'

'Give me two hundred rupees. Say he come after two week.'

Later, she also had the opportunity to see that precious luggage which had reinforced Sukurmani's belief that the carpenter would return.

The week after she was to leave for Thimphu.

'Sukurmani, I shall be going to Thimphu next week. There is no need for you to come to work for the time being. Here are five hundred rupees for you. Will you let me know when you have delivered? I don't know where you live; perhaps you could take me to your room one of these days.'

Sukurmani sat on the floor, staring blankly. Her soft skin had become dry; her face was devoid of any signs of makeup. She hadn't oiled her hair or even bothered to comb it. She had already stopped working in all the households for some time now.

Conversation between mother and son these days was limited to monosyllables of yes and no. Surju would finish whatever he was offered to eat without any fuss or preliminaries and rush out of the room. But a child is a child after all. Who would he throw his tantrums at if not his mother?

It was Sukurmani's duty to bring milk from the milkman, for which she paid her an extra fifty rupees. That day, Sukurmani's unusually hurried pace signalled that something untoward had happened. Surju was not with her.

'Memsaab, that...' she panted.

'What happened?'

'Memsaab, that milk ... Surju...'

Perhaps Surju had broken the bottle of milk.

'Memsaab, he sits on the road.'

Good heavens! Had the child hurt himself? Calamity never comes alone. 'Sukurmani, calm down and tell me what happened. Has Surju hurt himself on the way?'

'No Memsaab.' Then taking a deep breath, she finally blurted out the truth. 'Memsaab, the milk. I take it today. That Surju, he sits down on the road and cries. Says milk ... he want to drink milk. That money I give you...'

'Never mind. In any case I shall be leaving for Thimphu next week. You can take the milk while I am away.'

Milk was one of the rarities in Kanglung. There were very few Drukpas who owned cows in the town and even fewer who would sell milk. There was no other source of supply. Forget milk for drinking, a child like Surju would probably never even have tasted milk in Bhutan.

The journey from Kanglung via the lateral road to the capital Thimphu, a drive of five hundred and forty-seven kilometres, was a memorable one. The first stopover was at Trashigang, the district headquarters of Kanglung. Where was the district hospital located, she wondered. If Sukurmani was to be brought here for her delivery, the twenty-five-kilometre track from Kanglung to Trashigang was negotiable. But for the present she should concentrate on the picturesque view. Such a long journey for an expatriate was permissible only under this official programme, so she better make the best of this opportunity.

The main attraction of Trashigang was the seventeenth-century dzong or fortress built on top of a cliff right on the edge of town. Down far below was the river Dangmechu, one of the major tributaries of the river Manas in the east besides Kurichu and Tawangchu. All these rivers finally join the mighty Brahmaputra. The next stopover was at Mongar. The drive from Trashigang to Mongar, negotiating endless meandering curves and sharp turns, was really exhausting. Thirty kilometres from Mongar was Limithang and suddenly, there it was! The beginning of a series of huge waterfalls. The vegetation also changed dramatically. The barren, rocky mountains gave way to a lush green valley. Small poppy-like flowers grew in the grass; beautiful orchids hung from trees and foliage by the roadside, swaying in the breeze as if dancing. 'Don't pick or keep those flowers with you. You will feel nauseous,' warned the bus driver. What fine defense mechanisms nature possessed!

There is no night driving in Bhutan. For miles together we did not pass another vehicle on the way, nor did we see a single petrol pump or car workshop. This was similar to the barrenness of Kurichu; but in Kurichu there were at least some signs of human presence with those labourers on the construction site. The trees laden with bright multicoloured rhododendrons; the meadows visible in the far distance with horses grazing peacefully; the deep blue sky racing along with our bus; the snow-clad peaks immersed in silent conversation with the sky; specks of red, white and brown clouds scattered on the horizon in fantastic shapes and patterns; the gurgling streams flowing down the mountains—you had to bend your neck back like a bow from the bus window to appreciate this magnificent spectacle. This quiet solitary mortared road was the only connecting link between villages big and small, towns and cities. In the midst of this vast, awe-inspiring natural grandeur, this road was the only sign of human endeavour. Here and there on this long winding road one could see Indian labourers at work. Sukurmani had also worked on this same road at construction sites in Rungthung and Kurichu. The road remained where it was, bearing the weight of vehicles and travellers without complaint; a road after all is a road, you don't seek its permission to use it. But what about a living being who is reduced to a thoroughfare? Vehicles plying on the road are liable to pay toll for using it; but for the Sukurmanis of the world, where and on whom should the accountability be fixed?

Looking out of the window, she again made an attempt to divert her thoughts from Sukurmani to nature's grand panorama, but in vain. That petite figure staring with covetous eyes at the bus to Thimphu parked outside the gate of the lower market was transfixed in her mind; it brought a guilty lump to her throat. Off with Sukurmani! she firmly chided herself. When again would she be able to behold such a gorgeous pageant of white, pink, yellow and red rhododendrons!

Thrumsingla Pass at the height of 12,465 feet is the highest pass on this national royal highway. 'You are at the highest point' the roadside plaque announced. Nature and man united here to celebrate and salute God's creation. Small *tcshachas* or stupas stood in a row along with the colourful prayer flags fluttering in the wind; a stone structure and another chorten-like structure stood in silent prayer to the exotic pageant; the snow-clad highway, the broad leaves of tiny bonsai-like trees, all seemed mute witnesses to nature's infinite bounty.

In the conference at Thimphu there were impressive discussions and deliberations on many issues and topics of bilateral interest. But here, too, in the midst of all these participants and speeches, Sukurmani would make a silent, unobtrusive entry, sometimes alone, sometimes with Surju. That old habit of hers of never asking for anything, never speaking a word in her own defence; just silently standing there, wiping her hands with the same old tattered saree, her eyes on the ground. This really got on her nerves. Sukurmani, she wanted to scream, this is not an ordinary conference! You cannot trespass here. Here all the academics, bureaucrats and policy-makers are deliberating on important bilateral issues. A bilateral issue in simple terms means an issue of common interest and mutual cooperation between two countries. It is beyond your understanding and ability to make head or tail of these important discussions and debates. Here one talks about bilateral relations and areas of mutual cooperation. For instance, you could come to this country to work as a labourer only because of such cooperation between India and Bhutan, isn't it? As long as you worked on the roadside, weren't you paid wages? In an international conference of this kind there are deliberations on issues of internal and external security, technical cooperation and economic assistance. You and your son Surju are safe as long as our borders are safe and there is peace between the two countries. The mayhem and bloodshed in Kokrajhar or Darranga that forced you to migrate and the *himsa* you and your husband encountered are internal issues which have no place in a conference of this kind.

But, in a way, you do have a point. Had there been no mayhem and violence in Kokrajhar or Darranga, perhaps you would have remained in your village among your own people. You would not be in Rungthung or Kanglung as an illegal migrant running around without a work permit. You would not have to play hide and seek with the Bhutia officials and seek assistance from some Latif alias Basant to get the work permit. No Bihari or Bhutia would dare disturb you in the middle of the night, banging on your door and frightening your child. Life there amongst your own kinsfolk would have been different. If there were no violence in your country. Perhaps.

Bullshit. Words like if, but, perhaps all hang in the air like *trishankus*; they don't let you arrive at any decisive conclusion. Sukurmani was staring at her intently with anticipation and hope in her eyes: perhaps she could get a clue to Latif's whereabouts. Surely someone here in this important gathering might have seen the father of her unborn child in some part of Thimphu. If not his address, at least she could be provided a small hutment where no one would disturb her.

This was really most exasperating! How was she to concentrate on the ongoing deliberations if this woman stood there with that stoic expression on her face! She had never been so stubborn before. All right, Sukurmani, speak up. But be quick. What? Speak loudly. How can I convey your message if I don't hear you clearly? What? Surju, what...? Surju's admission to school, you mean? Yes, I get you. You wish to admit Surju to a school. I shall try and put forward your case, but I can't promise anything. It's not so easy. Our government has far more important and pressing tasks at hand than finding admission for the son of an illegal migrant in Bhutan. None of the children of your fellow labourers in Kurichu, Kanglung and Rungthung are going to school. So why are you so hell-bent on sending him to school? You don't want him to work on roads like you? And get two meals of rice a day. Yes, you would also like to travel to Mejguri once in a while to make short visits to your father. There, you and your son apprehend *himsa*. You have to come back to Kanglung in a truck. All these are extremely petty matters regarding bilateral relations or cooperation. And Sukurmani, listen to me carefully: next time you barge into a conference of this kind, do make sure to wear a clean saree at least. Now you better go out, don't just keep standing there at the entrance of the seminar hall.

In Thimphu they visited the India House. 'There you sing your national anthem, *Jana gana mana*,' the Drukpa escort joked. India House was one of the most impressive and grand buildings in the Bhutan capital. It was the month of May. The sprawling lawns of soft green grass and a dazzling array of flowers in full bloom were pleasing to the eye. In one corner of the palatial grounds was the huge mani run by the water mill, and there were a few swings. Oh no! Not again! She only had to think 'India,' and Sukurmani was back again—there she was at the threshold of the seminar hall, at least far from the view of the delegates, but here she had really crossed the limits. Ignorance is indeed bliss as they rightly say, or else how could Sukurmani have dared to barge inside the gates of India House? What does this illiterate woman know about etiquette, about social and political hierarchy? The bureaucrats at the Indian High Commission are no ordinary officers; they belong to the top echelons of society, and earn their passport for such coveted positions after years of hard work. All the work they do is of great import: meeting important people, attending important meetings, parties, functions. Our delegation could not get an audience with either the High Commissioner or even the First Secretary; they were both busy in some important meeting elsewhere. The list of complaints-cum-demands compiled with so much care after weeks of deliberations remained confined inside the pocket of poor Deepankar Ray, a young faculty at the college and the most energetic and enthusiastic of our group. Having had our fill of tea and biscuits in the High Commission hall, all the Indian teachers and delegates came out of India House. The junior officials there were generous enough to allow us to enter this huge building. Now tell me Sukurmani, whom could we have approached for the redressal of your grievances?

'God damn it! Babu Moshai was right. I shouldn't have come here!' Deepankar Ray was fuming with rage and indignation. She could empathise with him. He had taken great pains in drafting the contract teachers' representation which was to be submitted to the Indian High Commissioner, and was very hopeful that the Indian authorities at the Commission would redress the grievances of the long-term Indian teachers on contract.

'We all blame Babu Moshai for his sarcasm and his spoilsport attitude. But the truth always sounds harsh. This is precisely what he had been telling me all along—that these dialogues and interactions are all bullshit. Bloody trash. We contract teachers don't matter to them. None of us matters in fact. They are more than happy dining with Bhutan royalty, and will never turn their face eastwards as long as they are in office. But just a fortnight before their departure, they will visit the college on their way to the tour of East Bhutan. For the last twenty years, the contract teachers have been crying hoarse. Did anyone listen? I was an asshole to be so sanguine!' Ray's voice choked.

'Calm down *yaar*. I, too, am really frustrated. We all are. We didn't visit India House for that cup of tea and biscuits. This is what they call diplomacy. They are taught how to avoid and maintain a dignified distance from common folks like us. Where do we people find a place in the larger plans and policies of the nation state? Bilateral partnership, bonds of mutual friendship and cooperation my foot! Just empty, meaningless jargon. To hell with them! These last ten days we have been listening to them for nothing.' It was Dr. Rao.

'These people, these bureaucrats are the real cronies. Top class hypocrites. They are trained to develop a Narcissus-like fascination for themselves. I, me, myself; that's it. That old colonial mindset—keep away from the common gaze. Babu Moshai sounds cynical, but I will surely surpass his cynicism if I stay here for a few months more. Why would other nationals respect you when you don't respect your own people, don't protect the interests of your own countrymen? If an American or European dies or even gets hurt in any part of the world, the heavens would fall on the globe. That's what embassies and high commissions are for. Not like these cronies here who don't even have the decency to meet their own people on an official visit. They had been informed of our visit; the copy of the orientation programme was sent to them well in advance. This is what the *dasho* had assured me.' Ray's anger and bitterness was more than words could contain.

After their exit from India House, they passed by the office of the Indian Army. Where are you Sukurmani? Mark this—this is the topmost office of your GREF. Here there is a faint possibility of your complaint being entertained. Wiping her hands on her faded saree, Sukurmani silently stared at her. The constant unwanted presence of this woman, as if she were following her around everywhere, had an unnerving, dampening effect on her spirits; she felt gloomy and disinterested in everything.

It was the last day of the conference. The last session was an open session like the zero hour of Parliament. One could ask any question, direct or indirect, related to India and Bhutan. Everyone had come prepared for this session. Someone had not been paid their increment or not placed in the new pay scale. Life for many expatriate Indians in this country was confined to a mere contract, and even after serving in Bhutan for twenty years or more they had no future in terms of a career. Where would they find a job in India once their contract expired in Bhutan? There was boiling resentment amongst these old expatriates for the apathy of the Indian Government which, although the major donor country in Bhutan, preferred to remain silent on the cause of its own citizens. Once these individual personal concerns and interests had been voiced, other issues like the cross-border activities of the Bodos and ULFA and issues pertaining to other neighbours like Tibet, China and Nepal were included in these discussions.

All this while, Sukurmani stood silently at the entrance to the hall, fidgeting with the end of her saree, with Surju standing close by her side. She was neither inside, nor outside. She could not be framed into a supplementary question among the galaxy of questions. Amid all the issues of national and international importance related to China, Tibet, Nepal, the Bodos, and ULFA, a query related to a migrant woman labourer, that too an illegal one working on the roads constructed by GREF without a work permit, was invariably a petty, inconsequential query. While others were busy discussing the anomalies in pay scales and increments, renewals or extensions of contracts and so on, the issue of Sukurmani's work permit and wages could not simply be limited to a single question. After all, wasn't Sukurmani an inconvenient and messy bundle of neverending questions? One was allowed to ask one and only one question in this last session. Sukurmani, just let me know which question you would like to be represented by. A Dumka whose mother lost her life in some bloody clan skirmishes between the Santhals and Kukis, whose father had to flee as far as Mejguri in Assam to finally end up working as a water-carrier for the Bhutias. Every new generation has to bear the legacy of its ancestors; this is your legacy. This is the way of life. This is history. Today you inherit this destiny. Tomorrow Surju and the child in your womb will be the partakers of this destiny.

But, if you prefer, you could also be framed into another question: a single woman denied male protection. Though I am afraid this query might be turned down as a theoretical feminist paradigm and be earmarked for some women's commission instead. Nowadays, such gendered issues have lost their sanctity and often tend to be reduced to slogan-shouting and gimmickry of sorts. Every second woman today is overconscious about her 'self,' her identity and her individuality. Moreover, there are so many qualifiers attached to your womanhood: Dumka, tribal, poor, Darranga native, illegal migrant, wage earner, young, widow, single mother, pregnant. Sukurmani, you will have to select just one qualifier from all these specificities since one is allowed to ask only one question in this session.

But that taciturn, self-effacing woman just stood there, her gaze fixed on the ground, wiping her hands on her saree, with Surju holding on to her tightly.

It had been more than a week since her return from Thimphu, but there was no news of Sukurmani. She surely must have delivered by now. Was it a boy or a girl? Who knows even Latif might have come back. Kanglung is a small town; there are barely ten or twenty houses in all. She made some enquiries and finally in one house, she got Sukurmani's address. This was the first of the several visits she would make to the *quartar* where Sukurmani lived with Surju.

It was a small, dark, damp room and it stank. Sukurmani was lying on her back on the cot, her eyes open, gazing at nothing. She did not say anything when she saw her Memsaab, only followed her with her eyes; Sukurmani's woes never required the prop of tears or words. Here in this cramped room, for the first time in her life she encountered an extinguished hearth and Death waiting by the bedside. She had shopped to her fill in Thimphu; with the price she had paid for the carpets and wall hangings, this poor soul's life could have been purchased. She also surveyed Basant alias Latif's precious 'luggage' that had for so long sustained Sukurmani's hopes of his return: a kerosene stove, two plastic buckets without handles, a jute charpoy, a wooden table, few empty tins, four shirts hanging on a string, two pants hung on the peg and a pair of worn out slippers—all signs of a male presence in the room. She asked about the baby. By Sukurmani's account the delivery was overdue. Had the child then died in her womb? She must be taken to the hospital immediately; maybe she required surgery or needed to be given blood.

She rushed back home and requested her Drukpa neighbour to arrange for a vehicle immediately. Her neighbour replied, 'The vehicle will be arranged, but I shall not advise you to take her to the hospital. You know there is only one hospital in this area which caters to people from all the nearby villages. The biggest problem is that someone has to stay with the patient. Who will stay with Sukurmani in the hospital? There is also her son. The hospital discharges the patient immediately after delivery. Sometimes there can be post-natal complications. As you say, Sukurmani is very weak. How will you cope if she starts bleeding on the way? You will have to arrange for blood on your own. That winding, bumpy hill track of twenty-five kilometres, and in her condition ... you know how bad the road is. Heaven forbid, but what if she delivers on the way? Here in our place, deliveries are mostly done at home. You better look for a midwife instead.'

In the meanwhile, her Drukpa colleague from college arrived. 'What happened? Why this talk of hospital? Are you not well? I was wondering if we could go for our round of the market.' This colleague was her regular companion for the evening walk. When she told her about Sukurmani, she at once agreed to visit her.

Within half an hour they were in Sukurmani's room. Her colleague examined Sukurmani's abdomen and said, 'The delivery won't be due before a fortnight. If you really wish to help, let her not starve; give her good, nutritious food.'

She checked all the tins in the room standing in a row—all empty. She bought fresh replacements for those empty tins of food, but matters came to a standstill when it came to kerosene. It was not available in the whole market. She saw a pile of twigs and dried shrubs in the corner to be used as firewood.

'Surju brings them.' Leaning by the door, Surju cast a shy but eager glance towards them; their presence had enthused him into action. With great difficulty three litres of kerosene could finally be arranged. But was Sukurmani in a position to cook?

'Surju eats in Bathar's house. Surju also brings dry and damp firewood from here and there everyday.'

In the meantime she noticed that the door of the adjoining room, where Sukurmani's oft-mentioned Bathar lived, had been left ajar. On the facing wall hung a picture of Jesus Christ.

And so the mystery of this Bathar-Brother was at last resolved! Now all his assurances of free schooling, free food and medical care for Sukurmani and Surju made sense. 'Bathar's wife know delivery work.' Whatever had happened or was going to happen in Sukurmani's life courtesy this evangelising Christian Brother would be a hundred times better than Basant alias Latif's parting gift to her!

My Drukpa friend's prediction regarding Sukurmani was correct. Visiting Sukurmani twice a day in the mornings and evenings, she performed her *sakhi dharma*, a friend's duty. Surju's eyes would sparkle at the sight of Memsaab, who was sometimes accompanied by her Drukpa friend. He would always be standing at the door, waiting. And when he would catch sight of them he would rush inside to tell his mother about their arrival and then resume his position at the door.

And then one fine day, Sukurmani's child came into this world—a lovely little daughter.

'Amma says *bahini* comes.' Surju came to her house with the Brother's son Joseph to convey this news.

She recalled Sukurmani's words, 'There was no problem if Surju's bahini was there. Then she look after Surju. She would be as big as me. Then there was no problem. I know Memsaab.' And then her oft-repeated, 'He comes if it is a boy. I ask him when I meet him.'

The Brother's wife had delivered the child. The Drukpa landlord had condoned the rent for the room. With a bundle of clothes borrowed from her Drukpa friend she went off to see the little angel. 'There was no problem if Surju's bahini was there.' Blessing the child she prayed to God, please let it be true. May all the hardships, miseries and afflictions of Sukurmani come to an end with the birth of Surju's sister. May the shadows of her mother's woes never fall on this little soul. May the love and affection between the Dumka brother and his half-Muslim sister grow strong and be the harbinger of warmth, mutual empathy and friendship between different communities. Let other religious organisations also be informed about the networking of Sukurmani's Bathar. Be it in the name of religion only, let the fraternity of Surju Tutu and Surju Tutu's bahini be given access to free schooling, medicine, meals, a roof overhead and clothes to cover themselves so that the worries and troubles of the Sukurmanis of this world come to an end.

It was her last night in Kanglung. She was gripped by a mood of inexplicable melancholy and apathy. What do you say in English, the farewell blues. The things scattered all over the room reflected the state of her mind. For the last ten days she had been trying, in vain, to organise her belongings. But there were these remaining odds and ends which like a stubborn child refused to be put into any order. The piles of books, utensils, crockery, clothes and other titbits lying around the room waited patiently to be distributed or discarded. Right now she was confronted with the supreme challenge of packing all the necessary things in order of priority from these piles into one suitcase and one handbag. The entire room manifested the process of settlement vis-a-vis unsettlement. In just one day all the necessary and indispensible items collected and preserved with care over a year had suddenly turned useless and superfluous. Some of her colleagues had advised her to sell off these things. But over time objects of daily use also tend to acquire an emotional value and a life of their own, like children's toys. Can plants grown, watered and weeded with tireless patience and care be valued in terms of money? She had brought this hoe from the Japanese Agriculture Organisation at Khangma; the curtains she had sewn herself since she did not have a sewing machine; this handwoven carpet had been presented to her by one of her students.

At present all her necessities were compatible with the space in one suitcase and one bag. How was she to prioritise all these belongings in order of absolutely necessary, necessary and unnecessary from this motley assortment? What to take with her and what to leave behind? What she put into the suitcase and the bag would go back with her to India, the rest would be left behind. How to draw the line between sentiment and practical need? One part of her was filled with a sense of detachment—today she was parting ways with Kanglung; another day it would be the day of final reckoning. Right now she had the consolation of having a home to go back to, a job, familiar surroundings, her people, her country. But when she embarked on the final journey, the destination will not be known.

It was a peculiar state of mind she was in. She had fallen so much in love with this place and the people. Such affinity and ease she had not experienced even in her own land. She was going back to her own country where no entry permits or identity cards were required. She should be excited, elated; but on the contrary she was filled with a sense of gloom and indifference. She will have to start life all over again, set up her house from scratch. This relentless *chakravyuh* of life where everyone enters but very few know the exit point. Once more you join the race earmarked by the usual paradigms of 'development, progress and advancement.' Like the *jalkumbhi* or water hyacinth that grows and spreads surprisingly fast and effortlessly, choking lakes and ponds, and is useless to both man and animal, most of us are bound to join this mad race for progress. We crave the crown of fame, success and victory, but many have to reconcile with applauding the victory of some Alexander the Great and play second fiddle to one such victor. It could be any area of life: personal, social, professional or political. Either you become an Alexander, or be prepared to serve one. The choice is entirely yours, so is your effort and your destiny.

Far from the orchids and roses, the colourful *guldaudi* birds and chungas, the zangdopelries, manis and stupas, the prayer flags fluttering against an azure sky, the green forests, snow-capped peaks, valleys threaded by rivers and rivulets and the vast rich silence of nature, she would now have to retreat to a different, more urban world where there were mountains no doubt, but the vehicles plying on the roads cleaving the hills left no room to walk freely on the roads. Where there were temples, mosques and gurdwaras, but where the inner peace of the soul was lost in the cacophony of loudspeakers. That unforgettable panorama of nature on way to Thimphu, those huge cascading waterfalls, the endless turns on that solitary road, the fog and the clouds forming patterns in the sky, the steep slopes and ravines and those gorgeous rhododendrons of Bumthang Valley, would she ever behold them again? On the eve of parting, every object animate and inanimate seemed so intimate, so close to her heart.

It was dusk. The boys returning to college from the zangdopelri were visible on the road. She opened her window and watched them walk by in groups. Tomorrow when they would walk past this road, she would not be there to watch them. The room was filled with the intoxicating scent of wild roses and *rajnigandha*. From the curtainless windows, the red glow of the setting sun was visible on the horizon; the leaves of nearby trees and shrubs fluttered in the breeze. She would take this scene back home if it were possible. Then she would take with her these small colourful birds that hopped about in these shrubs.

Now she knew. The secret of the curtainless windows, the windows covered with faded, darned bedsheets, the chairs without cushions, the carpetless floors, the mats folded in a corner, the faded bedspreads and a handful of utensils in the kitchens of the senior Indian expatriates was now revealed to her. They were expatriates in the true sense of the word who, having realised the true meaning of 'temporary stay,' were leading their lives in a temporary way. There used to be much talk, repartee and jokes on temporary stay, temporary relationships and temporary contracts among the expatriate community; but like a novice swimmer she hadn't then dived into deep waters. Someone's term of contract was over; someone's contract was renewed; someone's contract was not renewed despite their wish and efforts; someone had been on contract for ten or twenty years—on all of them hung the same sword of temporariness. On average, there was one farewell party a month. Confronting this temporariness every moment of their life, these expatriate Indians had consequently turned apathetic to their surroundings and built shells around themselves. The older the expatriate, the greater the degree of his or her isolation and self-centredness. These passengers forever caught in transit, for how long could they bid other co-passengers farewell? Babu Moshai, Murlidharan, Daudi, how lonely this expatriation had turned out to be for all of them, like being exiled. Be they educated or illiterate, all expatriates were duty-bound or cursed to lead the expatriate life in their own way. Over and above everything, at the heart of her gloomy philosophical reflections loomed large the shadow of Sukurmani.

That afternoon she had gone to Sukurmani's room to say her final goodbye. Lying on the cot with her tiny daughter by her side, Sukurmani was staring blankly at the ceiling. Surju was standing behind the door as usual. At that moment, how desperately she wished she could prolong her stay, if only for the sake of this family. Within two-three months this woman would be strong enough to resume work.

'Sukurmani, I will be leaving Kanglung tomorrow. Take care of yourself and the children. Remember, you must be brave and strong. I know you *are* very brave and strong. Mrs. Mitra is still here. Sonam is also here. They will take care of you. So don't worry. I have left a few things for you. Sonam has promised to send them to you.' And putting some notes into Sukurmani's hand, she had walked out of the room.

After returning from that room a disturbing, disconcerting feeling of emptiness and unease seeped into her. She could not forget that blank, expressionless face of Sukurmani's. She had lost her near and dear ones so early in life, not once but so many times, while others, though alive, were as good as dead for her. Surju's baba, the father of the newborn child, Sukurmani's baba, her elder brother and her mother, Surju's elder sister—she had lost them all one by one. To be separated from her dear ones had become an inevitable part of Sukurmani's life, she had grown accustomed to it. What difference would it make to Sukurmani if this Memsaab too vanished from her life? But this knowledge gave her little consolation; it was nevertheless a vulnerable situation for Sukurmani and these two innocent children.

Suddenly the door bell rang. It could be her Drukpa neighbour; she had been invited to dine with them tonight. It was dark outside. She switched on the porch light and unbolted the door. Sukurmani stood there with her newborn daughter bundled in her arms. Surju stood close by her side in his familiar stance, staring at her intently.

'Sukurmani, *you*? I don't believe this! Why have you come out in this bitter cold with your newborn baby? Is everything all right?' she asked breathlessly.

'You go tomorrow, Memsaab.' The rest was conveyed by her smile.

'Come, come inside. Don't just stand there in the cold. Sit there on that mattress. Here, take this shawl and wrap the child with it. She'll catch a cold. Why on earth did you venture out with the baby in this cold!'

Clad in the yellow woollen baby suit gifted by her Drukpa neighbour, the infant looked like a little princess; Sukurmani looked more like her maid. The first fifteen days of this child in this world had passed reasonably well. There had been a surge of sympathy for the child in the entire female fraternity of Kanglung. Who knows, the stars of this newborn child might transform the fate of her mother and brother.

Handing over the baby to her son, Sukurmani promptly got down to helping organise the room. And Surju? Holding his bahini in his lap, he sat down on the mattress so comfortably as if he had been taking care of the little one all his life. In the blink of an eye her mood of unease, emptiness and gloom vanished, and the room was abuzz with activity and an air of bonhomie and camaraderie. This was the last day that the four of them would spend together in this room. Even if only for a few hours, the presence of the newborn was registered in this room. With the entry of Sukurmani's daughter in her house, the 'family' was now complete. From now on whenever she would think of Sukurmani, this happy picture would flash in her memory. It is customary to put oil on the head of a newborn on its first visit to a house or they say the house would be infested with mice. But she had no idea where the bottle of hair oil might be in this mess, and there was no threat of mice. She got up and took out the camera from her bag.

'Sukurmani, sit here on the mattress. Come closer to Surju and Gudia. Let's take a picture. I shall send it to you from India.' Sukurmani was smiling. So was Surju. God bless the three of them, she prayed from the bottom of her heart.

It was a priceless moment blessed with the dignity of motherhood. This dignity and power of motherhood could never render her children orphans, she believed. This last unexpected visit of Sukurmani had relieved her of her unease; an atmosphere of peace and joy emanated in the house. Setting her free from the burden of all anxiety, Sukurmani left for her home with the children. Without uttering a syllable, this taciturn woman had said everything.

If the story could have ended at this point, there would perhaps have been some satisfaction in concluding Sukurmani's saga on a somewhat positive, if not happy note. But what Professor Vinayak Singh shared with her cannot be omitted from this narrative.

That day she could not believe her eyes when she saw him walk into her office at the department.

'Professor Singh, you? Here? How come? Please take a seat. What a very pleasant surprise to see you here!'

'What do they say, the world is small. I thought why not refresh some memories of Kanglung with my old colleague.'

'When did you come back from Bhutan? Did you complete your term? Didn't you extend your term there?' She shot him several questions in one go. He had joined the college in Bhutan a year later than her.

'Yes, I did complete my term there but did not extend it. Not that I didn't want to. But you know all the hassles. My lien was not extended by my parent university. My services were found indispensible by my university and my department per se. I reached India only last month. I have come here to deliver a lecture in the refresher course.'

'I have been reading your articles on Bhutan, Dr. Vinayak. In one of your articles on the Bodo problem, you have raised some pertinent issues that need to be urgently addressed. While crossing Devthang, I, too, have thought along similar lines. I am happy that at least someone amongst us has put forth these issues in print. After all firsthand knowledge is always more authentic and substantive than secondhand information and reporting.'

'This is how you and I think, Professor Sahiba. I wish those in office also thought the same way. There are so many more such boiling issues that need to be seriously discussed and addressed. In the last few months you might have come across newspaper reports on the Bangladeshi labour force working in Bhutan. Once the construction work on the roads and bridges was over, these Bangladeshi labourers were dragged inside the Indian borders by the Bhutan Government.'

'Yes, the problem of the Bangladeshi labourers is a serious one. It is so difficult to distinguish between Indians and Bangladeshis on the grounds of appearance, language or dress.' She herself had mistaken that girl Pratima for a Bangladeshi until Sukurmani told her that she was from Kokrajhar. Sukurmani, too, could pass for a Bangladeshi.

'So Professor Sahiba, tell me how have you been doing? How does your reading and writing progress?' he enquired, switching to more personal things.

'It goes fine, but certainly not like it did in Kanglung. That kind of perfect ambience a writer seldom finds.' The natural landscape, the absolute silence and privacy of the cottage could turn anyone into a writer or a yogi. 'Do you know who came to stay in my cottage after I left? I really miss that cottage. Sometimes I even see it in my dreams.'

'You were the last illustrious occupant of that cottage,' Professor Singh replied with that hearty laugh of his for which he was famous, and which would give him away even from a distance. 'Wasn't that cottage once inhabited by the Canadian Jesuits? Who could be a worthier successor to it than you?' he said, still chuckling. The Bhutanese obsession with the white-skinned Canadians, Americans and Europeans was a constant butt of ridicule amongst the Indian community. While India was abridged to a terse GOI in all formal and informal references and conversation, the *gora* or white-skinned foreigners of all nationalities were profusely acknowledged and praised for what little help they offered Bhutan.

'Just joking. Soon after you left, the cottage was converted to a telephone exchange. Now all the teaching faculties have telephone connections.'

Time passed quickly once they were walking down memory lane, reminiscing the Kanglung days. It was already a quarter to two; Dr. Vinayak Singh's lecture was scheduled at two. Perhaps he could inform her about Sukurmani's whereabouts, but there was hardly any time now.

'Dr. Singh, do you remember there was a woman in Kanglung who worked for me? Her name was Sukurmani. She had a son called Surju. Later a daughter was also born to her.' And in an impulsive moment she opened her drawer, pulled out the bundle of papers and handed it over to Dr. Singh; Sukurmani's life story was penned down on these pages. Who would be a better reader and critic, the ideal *sahridaya pathak* or compassionate reader of this manuscript than a former colleague from Kanglung who, like her, was an eye-witness to many of the events and was familiar with several of the people in the narrative as well?

'Dr. Singh, this is my request: please give this a reading. I want your comments on it. Ever since my return from Kanglung, this woman has been uppermost in my thoughts. Sukurmani was not just a maid. She had been a companion and confidante in good times and bad. I shared a certain bond with her. What do we call it in theoretical terms, a bond of sisterhood. The evening before my departure, she came to my house with Surju and her fifteen-day old daughter. I have been anxious about her. I wonder how she must be coping with her two small children in a foreign land without a proper source of earning. Mrs. Mitra wrote to me that Sukurmani had picked up work with one or two houses in Kanglung. As you know Mrs. Mitra's term was over last year. Since then I have had no news of Sukurmani.'

'Yes, Sukurmani had also worked for me for some time,' said Dr. Singh and was about to elaborate further when one gentleman entered the room.

'Professor Sahiba, let me introduce Mr. Sahu to you. He has also come here to lecture in the refresher course like me. He has to meet a friend in the History Department. So now you must please excuse us. I will take your manuscript along with me to read and return it before I leave.' And both of them left the room.

She could not meet Dr. Vinayak Singh again. The next day she had to go to Delhi on an official assignment, and by the time she got back from Delhi, Dr. Singh had left. He had left the manuscript in the department office with the following note:

> Your Sukurmani saga is incomplete. I am adding the concluding note to it.
>
> After a few days of your departure for India, Sukurmani resumed work in some of the households. She told me that the grocery items and other things of daily use that you had left for her were of great help. It was indeed commendable how a handful of you women came together and took charge of Sukurmani and her children—what you aptly described as the bond of sisterhood. More than that, I think it was also a fine illustration of *matri shakti*, the power of motherhood. Motivated by your example, some of us men also engaged Sukurmani to work in our houses at a slightly higher pay, a hundred or two hundred rupees more than the normal

rate. Her son Surju, that child was a real artist—he would make such beautiful masks out of newspaper cuttings that you couldn't take your eyes off them! And he had a leadership quality in him. No game of the children in the colony was complete without Surju. He would also devotedly take care of his baby sister, carrying her around on his back in a sling while his mother worked.

And little Munni, there was such a tremendous lust for life in those tiny bright eyes, as if they proclaimed: I shall live and I shall overcome the sordid circumstances of my birth. Her shrill wails and whimpers would signal Sukurmani's arrival in the vicinity every day. Sometimes she would cry herself to sleep, and making the most of the opportunity Surju would quickly untie the knot of the makeshift sling and, laying Munni down at a safe spot, join his playmates briefly. When Munni would wake up crying, Sukurmani would shout for Surju, and he would promptly come and put his little bahini back in the sling with expert hands. Gone was his craze for copy and pencil. Mother and son had now teamed up with new energy and devotion to bring up little Munni. But once in a while Sukurmani would complain to me, saying, 'Memsaab give him copy, pencil and books. But Surju not study.' She was quite worried for Surju's education. She also tried several times to put him into school in Kanglung. I think it was this anxiety for his education that may have ultimately prompted her to move to Rungthung. One fine day, Sukurmani did not turn up for work. She had sent a new maid as her replacement, who told me that Sukurmani had left Kanglung and gone to Rungthung.

Something seemed to have been troubling Sukurmani for some time. Had you or Mrs. Mitra been there, perhaps she could have confided in you. But men have their limitations and boundaries with regard to such issues. That she found it difficult to meet living expenses or something to that effect she had once admitted to me. Another major cause of her anxiety was the work permit; her illegal status put Sukurmani in a very vulnerable position, as you of course know. Then she was frequently harassed by the local Assamese and Bengali men working for Drukshiring. Presumably fed up with all these everyday hassles, she decided to leave Kanglung. After all who was there in Kanglung to support her? The lure of Surju's schooling could also have been a decisive factor for her. As the new maid told me, Surju joined school in Rungthung; for a few months he was taken to school to get acquainted with the new enviroment with the help of someone.

It was rumoured that this someone was Sukurmani's fourth man, her last predator. No one had a clue as to who this man was. Some said he had recently converted to Christianity. I am sure you know that the Christian missionaries were quite active in these labour camps. While Sukurmani was still in Kanglung, a man had once come as far as my house, making enquiries about her. He claimed to be an old acquaintance of hers and said he had come to meet her from Rungthung. From his speech he sounded like a Bihari. Maybe he was the one. I do not know. Whoever he was, I learnt later that Sukurmani passed away under mysterious circumstances. It seemed she had been sick for some time and life certainly couldn't have been easy for her with two small children. There was no one to take care of her. Someone said she had consumed some poisonous herbs in an attempt to get rid of the unwanted foetus in her womb, which proved fatal. She must have taken something from some local apothecary. We don't doubt her intentions; this woman betrayed by two ruffians rightly thought of terminating the unwanted pregnancy. But her death changed the meaning of life for her two children overnight.

For a few days Surju remained in Rungthung with Munni. The two orphans might have been offered meals for a few days out of sympathy for their recent bereavement. Then I heard that the labourers of Rungthung and that fourth man registered a complaint in the GREF head office against them and got rid of the two. One fine day the two children were bundled across the Indian borders adjacent to Mejguri village in a GREF vehicle. What happened to them thereafter I do not know. There is every possibility that they might have been picked up by the Christian missionaries and were taken care of. There was one Christian priest who visited them occasionally when their mother was alive. We can only hope that the two reached a safer place than Rungthung.

It grieves me deeply to convey this sad ending to your narrative, as I know it must grieve you. But then the quintessence of life is to know and accept the truth. On the testimony of faith in humanity and belief in God, you and I can only pray with folded hands and

> wish for a happy, fairytale-like turning point in the lives of Surju and Munni.'
>
> V. Singh

Let it be true. God bless them wherever they are. Let them be in safe hands. Let there be a happy, fairytale-like turning point in the lives of Surju and Munni.

Some years ago she had penned a letter to Sukurmani's father Sarju Tutu. Although the fate of that letter or its intended recipient was not known, since no reply ever came, the letter played a catalyst's role in initiating a bond between memsaab and maid. And now once more she was writing a letter, this time for Sukurmani's son, Surju Tutu. The last time when she had acted as letter-writer for Sukurmani, there was much less involvement on her part; the words, thoughts and sentiments were those of Sukurmani. But this time it was different. In absence of the real actor, the onus of conveying the thoughts, wishes and sentiments of the absent actor had fallen on her.

Time and tide wait for no one; the brother and sister would have grown up by now. Unlike his bahini Munni, Surju had spent the precious first few years of his life with his mother; he may still retain some memories of his pre-orphaned childhood days in Bhutan when mother and son shared breakfast every morning, and he followed her around like a shadow. What memories must Surju cherish of those early days? Who must he blame for the turn of events in his and his sister's life? Sooner or later, that insurmountable question of accountability is likely to crop up in his mind. And when it does, Sukurmani will not be there to present her side of the story.

Dear Surju Tutu, this letter is for you. You need to know certain things about your mother, of her heroic struggles and ordeals to which this Memsaab was an eye-witness. All through her life this wronged woman never uttered a word of protest in her defence. While Sukurmani was alive, this Memsaab could not be of much help to her despite best intentions. On Sukurmani's behalf, she would like to put in a few words. Perhaps also as a means of atonement. In the gamut of fixing accountability, this Memsaab, too, is a culprit. In her hour of crisis, she, too, failed Sukurmani and finds herself on the side of Sukurmani's predators.

What has passed is past and cannot be changed. But revisiting the past enables you to re-view reality from an objective perspective. The truths hidden from sight are of greater consequence than surface reality. The dignity and enigma of the movement of an iceberg is that only one-tenth of it is visible on the surface, Ernest Hemingway once said. A retrospective revisit of the life of the woman named Sukurmani, whose real name was Hujunmoi, will enable you to see her with different eyes, and make you feel immensely proud of your mother.

She gave you, a fatherless child in a foreign land, an identity and a place in the world by giving you her own father's name—your last name Tutu is your ancestral identity, your maternal grandfather's name and the talisman your mother protected you with in a harsh world. She left Kanglung for Rungthung for your sake because she desperately wanted to put you in school, to educate you, to see her son grow up as a responsible and proud citizen of his country, his des. She did not want you to remain an illiterate labourer and an illegal migrant's son. Do you know she had a fabulous vocabulary of more than half a dozen languages including English?

The entry of Munni's father in her life was also because she wanted you to have a father figure to look up to. She had high goals and ambitions for you; she wanted a different life for you. Surju, when you remember your mother, you must also remember her great struggle against tremendous odds and her many untold sacrifices. In her brief but eventful life, every day brought new challenges, and your mother always confronted them head-on without much ado. She had pride; she never begged for help and she never saw herself as hapless or helpless.

Bygones are bygones and one cannot change them. Dear Surju, this story is for you. I believe that Sukurmani's dream for you and her many sacrifices to educate you were not in vain, and wherever you may be today, that you and your bahini can read this letter.

Glossary

arra: A home-brewed alcoholic drink usually distilled from barley or wheat.

chorten: A reliquary mound in the shape of a closed, stone-walled structure without any doorway or entrance. Throughout Bhutan, chortens or stupas line the roadside, marking the spot where Guru Padmasambhava or Zhabdrung may have stopped to meditate. Young and old, men and women of all ages can be seen circumambulating these chortens. There are eight types of chortens; all eight can be found in the Gompa near Phuntsholing built by the royal grandmother in the reign of Jigme Dorji Wangchuck (1952–1972). But the most common chorten found in Bhutan is called *khangtseg* or the house chorten, which anyone can build and which is considered an act of great piety. Relics in the form of liturgical texts, corals, precious stones, metals, grain, fabric, cash and coins may be preserved in various parts of the shrine.

dasho: An official title for a man; a dasho is entitled to wear the red scarf unlike other men who wear the white scarf.

dhar: Colourful Buddhist prayer flags in red, green, white or yellow with specific prayers inscribed on them for avoiding calamity or nullifying the effect of bad stars in the horoscope. It is obligatory for a Bhutanese to erect fourteen prayer flags in the event of a death in the family.

drubchen: The annual festival of worship introduced in Bhutan by Zhabdrung Rinpoche, considered to be the founder and father of the Bhutanese nation, and later popularised by Terton Rigzen Jatshen. It includes elaborate rituals and colourful mask dances performed inside the zangdopelri for the purification of the locality and is concluded with the blessing ceremony.

Drukpa: The Bhutanese people.

Druk Yul: The Land of the Peaceful Dragon or Land of the Thunder Dragon, as Bhutan is also called.

dzong: A monastery fortress. Until the beginning of the twentieth century, Bhutan was ruled by the dual system of administration known as *chhosi* initiated by Zhabdrung Ngawang Namgyal, or Zhabdrung Rinpoche as he is popularly known, in 1651. The twin administrative and religious bodies are still housed together in the dzong. The *dzongda* is the district administrator of the dzong, while the *lam neten* is the chief abbot of a *rabdey* or the monk body of a district. The Trongsa Dzong built by Zhabdrung in the seventeenth century is the biggest dzong in Bhutan, and also the royal family's ancestral home.

gho: An outfit worn by men, also known as *baku* in Nepali, this is a long robe tied around the waist by a specially made belt of cotton or woollen fabric. The folds in the front of the robe are used as a pouch for carrying things. The material commonly used is a homespun chequered cloth called *matha*.

kira: A long robe worn by women reaching from the shoulders to the ankles, secured at the shoulder with a silver or gold brooch and tied at the waist by a broad belt, which is usually much broader than that worn by men. A long-sleeved blouse known as *wanju* or *khenja* is worn inside while over the kira a long-sleeved silken, synthetic or cotton coat known as *tego* is worn.

lhakhang: A Buddhist temple.

mani: A rotating prayer wheel.

Sharchopa: The local dialect of Eastern Bhutan; *sha* means east.

tcshacha: A small chorten.

tshechu: An important religious festival of Bhutan. The Drukpas believe that the Buddha took rebirth on earth as Guru Padmasambhava, and his day of birth is held to be the tenth day of the sixth month of the Bhutanese calendar. The tenth day of every month of the Bhutanese calendar is also observed as the Great Guru's day and is called 'Tshechu' which means 'the tenth day.' All the tshechus in the provincial capitals are celebrated on the tenth day of the Bhutanese month.

zangdopelri: Literally meaning the heavenly abode of Guru Padmasambhava, it is a temple devoted to the Guru.